MASCOT BOOKS

www.mascotbooks.com

Hey, Brother

©2018 A.J. Stewart. All Rights Reserved. No part of this publication may be reproduced, stored in a retrieval system or transmitted in any form by any means electronic, mechanical, or photocopying, recording or otherwise without the permission of the author.

This is a work of fiction. Names, characters, businesses, places, events, and incidents are either the products of the author's imagination or used in a fictitious manner. Any resemblance to actual persons, living or dead, or actual events is purely coincidental.

For more information, please contact:
Mascot Books
620 Herndon Parkway, Suite 320
Herndon, VA 20170
info@mascotbooks.com

Library of Congress Control Number: 2018902085

CPSIA Code: PROPM0118A
ISBN-13: 978-1-68401-681-5

Printed in the United States

Above all else, be kind.

A.J. Stewart

Hey, Brother

A.J. Stewart

For my brother,
you dick.

Hey brother! There's an endless road to rediscover
Hey sister! Know the water's sweet but blood is thicker
Oh, if the sky comes falling down, for you
There's nothing in this world I wouldn't do
Hey brother! Do you still believe in one another?
Hey sister! Do you still believe in love? I wonder
Oh, if the sky comes falling down, for you
There's nothing in this world I wouldn't do
What if I'm far from home?
Oh brother, I will hear you call!
What if I lose it all?
Oh sister, I will help you hang on!
Oh, if the sky comes falling down, for you
There's nothing in this world I wouldn't do

—Avicii, "Hey, Brother"

Chapter One

The dog heard it before they did. He lifted his head, ears pricked, and let out a low growl. Hackles raised, Nuke barked once. A warning.

"Shh..." Jane whispered, rubbing his ears to calm him.

Jane turned in the direction Nuke was facing. She couldn't see anything but bare trees and dense laurel bushes. Willa looked up from her wash tub and met her sister's gaze, eyes wide. Jane nodded toward the trees on the far side of their little clearing, then slipped on her sneakers. She grabbed her bow and quiver and scaled the tall oak she had been leaning against. The fact that the branches didn't start until ten feet up didn't faze her. Willa darted into the tree line on the other side of the little clearing they had been calling home. At the back of the clearing, their horses snorted and stomped.

Jane kept close to the tree trunk. The branches, with their dead, brittle leaves, barely quivered beneath her deft feet. Even the squirrels were surprised by her sudden and noiseless appearance. About twenty feet up, she found a sturdy perch and nocked an arrow onto her bow. Only then did she glance around; Willa was behind a gnarled oak, pistol drawn.

Willa caught Jane's gaze and gave a little nod, *Do it.*

Jane whistled a tittering bird call and waited for the telltale response. Seconds passed in silence. Jane pulled the bowstring tighter and tighter, waiting for the answering whistle that meant all was okay.

Heavy, crashing footsteps in the woods made her heart leap into her throat. It was loud enough to startle, but not near enough to see.

Nuke started barking. Keeping her arrow trained in the direction of the noise, Jane stole a glance at Willa. She had both hands around her pistol, her expression hardened.

Jane whistled again, finally receiving a response, but it was not the bird call she was expecting.

A strong, exasperated male voice rang out through the trees. "I hear you, dammit! Stop whistling, Jesus Christ..."

Jane relaxed her bow and rolled her eyes, letting out the breath she didn't realize she was holding. Nuke's barks became excited yelps as a large man astride a massive black horse emerged from the tree line.

He was a Herculean man with a wild, unkempt beard and bright eyes brimming with mischief. Nuke yapped and danced in crazed circles around Max's legs. His bushy tail whirled around and around, like a helicopter building up momentum. The horse snorted in annoyance.

"You're supposed to whistle back, you ass," Willa admonished as she holstered her pistol and strode across the clearing.

"I would have if I could remember what the tune was. Get down, Nukem." He swatted at the dog, which was nosing at the furry bundle in his lap.

Jane climbed down the tree. She let go and fell the last few feet, landing with hardly a grunt in front of her brother. She pushed her short curls back behind her ear and smiled.

The relief she felt that it was Duke, and not another thief, was short-lived. Duke's shirt was soaked in blood and he held his left arm awkwardly against his chest as he reined in Max, his massive black Percheron. Having once pulled carriages down in Savannah, Georgia, Duke had named him Duramax, because "with all that pulling power, he has a lot of bottom end torque."

At twenty-six, Duke was the youngest of the three of them. He always rode with an air of pride, head high and barrel chested. So it was odd to see him slumped over in an awkward position.

"What the hell happened?" Willa asked as she and Jane rushed forward to help. Duke had a large deer draped across Max's rump and a large furry...something in his lap.

"Found this pained expression in the closet," he grimaced, "and thought I'd try it on. How does it look?"

"Not nearly as good as that strappy little number you had back in Pensacola." Jane's reply was deadpan as she pulled the furry mass from his lap. On closer inspection she realized it was a bobcat. She handed it to Willa, who took it to hang from a tree, out of reach of scavenging animals.

"Oh c'mon, that was one time!"

Willa laughed. "I remember that. A little black one with sequins. What was her name?"

Jane affected a smoldering look and a smoky voice. "It was Jasmine."

Duke shuddered. "I'll never look at a blonde the same way again."

Jane and Willa laughed again.

Duke swung his leg over Max's back. He made a valiant attempt to land gracefully, but with only one good arm to balance with, he slid awkwardly from his saddle. He hit the ground with an anguished grunt; his knees buckled slightly under his heavy landing. Leaning on Jane, he let her lead him to their campfire and sat down. He ran his hand through his hair. Usually cropped close to his scalp, his hair had grown out into a wild crown of curls. It had been a while since any of them had had a proper haircut. Willa was the only one that missed out on the curly hair gene. Her dark brown hair hung in loose waves around her shoulders as she bustled around, gathering supplies for Jane.

"So what happened?" Willa asked.

"Me and Sylvester over there had a disagreement over Bambi," he explained as Jane cut away his shirt. "Aww man, I liked this shirt."

Having strung up the deer, Willa approached with a bucket of water and a bundle of rags. She retreated, determined not to look at the bloody mess. Even after all these years, she still couldn't stand the sight of blood.

"Naturally, I won the argument," Duke continued proudly.

"Naturally," Jane agreed distractedly. His shoulder had been ripped to shreds. Considering the copious amounts of blood that soaked his shirt, he had come pretty damned close to losing the argument.

Jane, the eldest, began to rinse the wound and dab at it with a rag. As the dirt and blood was cleared away, the severity of it became more pronounced. Three deep gashes sliced across his left shoulder and down his chest. There was a knot on the end of his shoulder. It wasn't as bad as she expected but still bad enough to warrant professional attention.

Jane did pretty well tending to their medical needs for the most part. Between the three of them, they had had more stitches than Frankenstein's monster over the past three years, most of which Jane had sewn herself. Not to mention the countless broken fingers and toes, dislocated joints, and the inevitable scrapes and bruises. But these claw marks would need more than fishing line stitches and a fifth of whiskey. This would need sterile bandages, antibiotics, and maybe a tetanus shot. None of which she had.

"This needs stitches," she said vaguely.

As if on command, Willa appeared at her side with the medical kit. Jane waved her hand ambiguously. Willa put down the kit and walked away.

"I think it's dislocated, too," Duke said.

Jane opened the bottle of hydrogen peroxide, not looking him in the eye. "I am aware of that."

She doused the wound in peroxide. Duke hissed as it bubbled and stung.

"Ready?" Jane asked.

"Ready for what?" Duke was confused and suspicious.

Jane doused his shoulder again. Distracted by the sting of the antiseptic, he was too late in realizing that Jane's hands were pressed against his collarbone, while two more hands gripped the back of his shoulder. Before he could resist, Jane said, "Now!" And the two pairs of hands pushed in opposite directions, forcing his shoulder back into place. Duke bellowed in pain and surprise. Willa came around from behind and started pulling fishing line out of the medical kit for his stitches while Jane returned to cleaning the gashes.

"What the hell was that?" Duke demanded.

"Oh hush, you big baby," Willa scolded. "You always tense up. It's easier to pop back in when you're not tense."

Duke glared at her, and then yelped as Jane pricked him with her sewing needle.

"Jesus Christ, ya'll," he cried as Jane threaded the line through his skin.

"It's easier when you're not tense," Jane repeated.

Duke sighed and ceded the argument. "You two are going to be the death of me." He yelped again as Jane continued to thread the fishing line through his ragged flesh. Once he stopped yelling, Nuke came over and laid his head in Duke's lap.

"Can you believe them?" He looked down at Nuke. "A couple of pecking hens, ain't they?"

Nuke looked up at Duke. He seemed to be saying, *Well, what did you expect?*

Jane continued to stitch her brother's shoulder as he bickered with Willa, who was trying to salvage what she could of his shirt.

"Do you really have to cut up my shirt?" he whined.

"Jane already cut it in half. What do you expect me to do? Sew it back together?"

He shrugged.

"I am not going to sew it back together. You've got other shirts."

She cut away the bloody parts and cut the rest into strips. After the shirt-turned-bandages were washed, Jane wrapped them around his shoulder. Willa dug through Duke's stuff, looking for more laundry.

"Hey! Get out of my stuff!"

"I'm doing laundry."

"What does that have to do with my stuff?"

"I'm just looking for clothes. Chill out. Just thought you might have a loose sock or something crammed down in your pack."

"Trust me, if I had a sock crammed down in my pack, you would not want to wash it."

"That's disgusting, Duke. Ew!"

"Then don't touch my stuff."

Willa went back to the laundry she was working on, while Jane and Duke set about gutting the deer and bobcat. Nuke sat at their feet, watching their every move, licking his lips. Jane was not totally unaware that Duke and Willa were having an animated but silent conversation while she wasn't looking. Finally, Duke broke the awkward silence.

"I'm going to need antibiotics," he said.

Jane didn't reply.

"We need to go into town," Willa ventured.

No reply.

"Oh c'mon. Don't act like you don't know where we are," Willa said.

She was right. Jane knew exactly where they were, just off of highway 441, just outside of Dillsboro, North Carolina. Only a two-day ride from the one place Jane had not seen in three years. Duke was right, too. The gashes in his shoulder were too deep. Too dirty. Infection was inevitable if it wasn't properly sterilized. And that was something Jane couldn't do down here in the woods. He needed a doctor, and the closest one was in Cashiers Village.

Jane sighed. "Yeah. I know." She pulled the hide from the deer. "We'll leave in the morning. We need to finish preparing these animals first, and it's already close to three o'clock."

Her siblings agreed. As the days crept closer to October, their hours of sunlight dwindled. Jane continued to butcher the animals the best she could, while Duke rubbed down his horse. It was a tough job, even with two hands, but Duke was just proud enough to insist that he didn't need help.

They packed up their belongings so they would be ready when they got up in the morning. Once everything was packed, it would only take a few minutes to load it onto their pack mule, Jack. Ornery and prone to biting if you got too close while he was eating, Jack had nonetheless been a valuable addition to their little caravan. Duke took a package out of his saddle bag and moved to stash it in one of Jack's packs.

"No way," Willa stopped him. "That goes in your saddle bag."

"But I don't have room for it!"

"We told you that when you found it. Jack is for carrying group stuff only. Personal stuff goes in your saddle bag. It's not our fault you stuffed your bags full of tannerite and fireworks. You made it fit before. You can make it fit now."

Duke had an affinity for things that go *boom*. When he found a small stash of explosive material at an abandoned house, he couldn't help himself. He scowled at Willa but took the package of tannerite back to his saddle bag and set to trying to reorganize everything.

They had been camped in their little clearing for three days. They had hoped to stay a little longer but it was just as well. They were uncomfortably close to the Blue Valley Boys' territory. It wouldn't be long before the Valley Boys found them anyway. And since they had to cross straight through Valley Boy territory to get to Cashiers Village, a meeting with the Valley Boys was inevitable. Jane wanted it to be on her terms.

Her breath hitched in her chest when she thought about having to deal with them again. She had been on good terms with many of them, but they were still a rough and dangerous group. Despite her nerves, a spark of excitement lit up inside her and she smiled.

Chapter Two

Willa nudged Jane in the back with her foot.

"Get up."

Jane groaned and rolled over. "Five more minutes." Her reply was muffled by the threadbare blanket she pulled over her head.

Willa nudged her again. "You said that fifteen minutes ago. Get up. We got a lot of shit to do today." Nukem joined the nudging, poking his wet nose under the blanket.

Eyes clenched shut against the clear, bright dawn, Jane sighed. Willa yanked the blanket away. Jane groaned in childish protest. In spite of the years of living dawn to dusk, Jane was still not a morning person. Today, in particular, morning had come much too soon, sleep had not come soon enough. Awake half the night with her thoughts, Jane felt like she had not slept at all.

She rolled over and sat up, rubbing her face. It was a cool, crisp morning. The bright sunlight filtered through the leaves that were beginning to fade from green to yellow. Squirrels chattered to each other in the branches overhead as they prepared for the coming cold. The scent of cooked meat and apples permeated the air. It was late September, but Jane couldn't remember the date exactly.

Willa pressed a warm tin cup of coffee into Jane's hands. Just the smell of coffee woke her considerably. It had been months since she had smelled its warm, spicy scent. They only had one small bag of it, and they had been saving it for a time like this. The grogginess faded as she took a sip, then gagged at the taste.

"See, I told you it was bad," Duke laughed. Jane looked up at him. He was packing their sparse belongings onto their pack mule, Jack. He reached up to tie the top but winced when he stretched his stitches. Willa rolled her eyes and went to help him.

"Oh shut up," Willa snapped. "It is not that bad."

Duke looked at Jane inquiringly.

Jane shook her head. "It's okay." Jane took another tentative sip but she could not completely hide her wince.

Duke roared with laughter. "Tastes like battery acid, don't it?"

"Alright, smartass, next time you can try making coffee with grounds that expired two years ago...dick," Willa replied.

Willa went back to the campfire where she had their cook pot simmering with venison from the deer Duke brought back last night and apples from a nearby tree. She ladled out a heap of it onto a tin plate and handed it to Jane. It tasted a hell of a lot better than the coffee and Jane scarfed it down. Jane fed a piece to Nukem.

While she ate, Willa cornered Duke.

"Sit down," she commanded.

"Why?" He looked at her sideways.

"Because you can't be trusted to actually take it easy with your shoulder. So I'm going to do it for you."

She held up a wide roll of Ace bandages. After some cajoling, bickering, and name calling, Duke's arm was securely tied to his side.

"You didn't have to make it so tight," he whined.

"Oh yes I did. It'll be harder for you to work it loose. Same reason why the knot is in the back."

Duke flailed around trying to reach the knot with his free hand.

Once they had all eaten, the three of them saddled their horses and broke camp. They rode at a comfortable pace down the highway for several hours. Nukem pranced alongside them, occasionally disappearing into the trees to chase a squirrel. The closer they came to the intersection with Highway 107, the more Jane's anxiety rose. It was more than just butterflies in her stomach. It was like panicking grasshoppers in her chest.

Jane thought about what they had to do next, trying to stay a couple of steps ahead. There would probably be at least two Valley Boys stationed at the intersection, maybe more. She had been on good terms with them in the past. Some of them had been her friends. But that was a long time ago. If they had taken on new people, people she didn't know, then there could be problems.

Jane carried on a lively, if forced, conversation with Willa and Duke; lighthearted banter that made it obvious to anyone listening that they were not a threat and, more importantly, they weren't trying to hide. That they weren't afraid. The conversation served another purpose for Jane. It helped calm her anxieties when she had other things to occupy her mind.

Duke rambled on about football. Again. "The pass rush in '15 was unbelievable. Freakin' Jared Allen, man. Led the league in sacks. The defense forced a shit ton of turnovers. Cam may have been NFL MVP, but it was that badass defense that got 'em to the Super Bowl."

Whenever Jane and Willa let him, that was all he talked about. He could go on forever about the Panthers, or his own team, Appalachian State. Most of the time, Willa and Jane would try to steer the conversation in another direction, but today Jane was too preoccupied to pay much attention.

After a while, there came a lull in the conversation. When you spend every waking moment with the same people, for years at a time, you tend to run out of things to talk about. Duke could sense that Jane's attention was beginning to wander. He knew it would just lead her back to her anxiousness. He, much more than Willa, was in tune with her mental state and could sense subtle changes in her mood. Duke knew just the thing to help bring her back from the brink. He started to sing.

> *One evening as the sun went down, and the jungle fires were burning*
> *Down the track came a hobo hiking, and he said, 'Boys, I'm not turning.'*

I'm headed for a land that's far away, beside the crystal fountains
So come with me, we'll go and see the Big Rock Candy Mountains.

Jane tried, and failed, to suppress her grin. Duke smiled back and sang louder.

In the Big Rock Candy Mountains, there's a land that's fair and bright
Where the handouts grow on bushes, and you sleep out every night
Where the boxcars all are empty, and the sun shines every day
Oh the birds and the bees and the cigarette trees, the lemonade
Springs where the bluebird sings, in the Big Rock Candy Mountains.

She rolled her eyes and joined him.

In the Big Rock Candy Mountains, all the cops have wooden legs.
And the bulldogs all have rubber teeth and the hens lay soft boiled eggs.
The farmers trees are full of fruit, and the barns are full of hay.
Oh I'm bound to go where there ain't no snow,
Where the rain don't fall and the wind don't blow
In the Big Rock Candy Mountains.

Their singing died as they approached the barrier at the intersection. There were two men manning the barricade. One had a revolver pointed at them. The other seemed reluctant to aim his rifle at them and aimed at their knees instead. They were not any of the Valley Boys that she knew. If fact, they weren't Valley Boys at all.

"Hold it right there," the man with the revolver demanded.

He was lanky, with a dirty bandage around his elbow. He looked like he'd recently shaved with a dull knife and butchered the job. Jane pulled her horse, Mahz, to a stop. Duke and Willa stopped on either side of her, a few steps behind. Nukem bristled and growled.

"I'll need ya'll to come down off them horses," left man said. He strutted out toward them like he owned the place. His partner hung back and didn't say anything. His skin was sallow around gaunt eyes that were empty and emotionless. It was obvious he was a drug addict. Thin as a twig, he trembled like a Chihuahua.

"I think we'll stay where we're at, thanks," Jane said calmly, "but we have this bobcat that we would be happy to trade for safe passage."

It seemed easier to let the men believe they were in control of the situation. Better to avoid conflict if they could.

"The cat will be enough for the big man, but the ladies, I think, will require a bit more payment." His tone was shady and sinister.

Left man approached Willa mounted on her horse. Several hands slipped unnoticed to weapon hilts.

"I would rethink that, if I were you," Duke said. In this tense moment, Duke seemed unnaturally calm. Willa looked at the man in disbelief.

The man sneered at Duke. "And what exactly do you think you going to do?"

"Oh, I'm not going to do anything." Duke leaned back in his saddle and scratched the underside of his beard.

"Damn right, you ain't." He turned and leered at Willa and placed his hand on her knee. Nukem growled.

Willa reacted instinctively. She kicked her foot out of the stirrup and planted it as hard as she could in his face. Howling in pain and shock, he gripped his face. Blood gushed from his shattered nose, through his fingers.

"You got-damn bitch!" He raised his revolver in his free hand but before he could pull back the hammer, two other pistols clicked into place and leveled on him. Jane drew back her bow string. The tweaker yelped in surprise. His rifle clattered on the pavement as he ducked behind the barrier.

Duke grinned smugly. "I told you to rethink that idea."

"You wanna start this conversation over?" Jane asked.

"Shit, man!" The man had a pitiful, pleading edge in his voice now. "We's just tryin' to get by and survive. Same as ya'll. A man's gotta do what he's gotta do, right?"

"And raping women is necessary to your survival, is it?" Jane asked.

"Aw, c'mon now, you know I wasn't serious. Just a joke, was all!"

"Oh yes, hilarious," Willa replied. She slid from her saddle and strode over to the man, holding her gun to his head. Still clutching his nose, he backed away from her and tripped over the rifle. He sprawled to the ground.

The tweaker leapt out of the way, hands in the air. "I swear, I didn't have nuttin' to do wit it. All his idea. I ain't got no use for rapin' nobody. I'm just here because he said he'd help me score some dope. I swear to God, I just wanted some dope. Please don't kill me."

"It's alright," Jane said. She and Duke had joined Willa on the ground. "We're not going to kill you. We don't take lives if we don't have to."

Duke cuffed the man with duct tape and sat him down against the barrier. He started to yell and curse and fight his bonds. "Ya'll are in deep shit now. Don't you know who I am? I am Emory Howell. I am a very important person in the Blue Valley Boys. You have messed with the wrong man. I swear to God, I will make sure all three of you hang for this!"

Willa kneed him in the head, knocking him over. "Oh shut up, you sorry sack of shit."

The addict looked back and forth between the three of them, clearly afraid of being cuffed and kicked like his comrade. "What are you gonna do to us?"

"Us? What do you mean, 'us?' There ain't no 'us' anymore, you got-damn traitor. Look what they done to me, and you ain't got shit." Emory continued to yell and thrash.

Willa kicked him again. Jane turned to the tweaker. "What's your name, hun?" Her voice was soft and reassuring. The addict relaxed.

"Leonard."

"Leonard, I'm Jane. This is my sister Willa, and my brother, Duke." Jane extended her hand to him. Tentatively, still slightly terrified of her and her siblings, he shook her hand.

"Here's what's gonna happen, Leonard. You got a camp somewhere?" Leonard nodded. "Good. You're gonna take Duke to your camp, bring back anything of value, then we're takin' you and your buddy here to the Blue Valley Boys. If you'll do that for us, I'll make sure you're taken care of."

Leonard smiled, but Emory exploded.

"That's bullshit, and you know it Leonard. I'm part of the Valley Boys. I told you that. This bitch is makin' promises she can't keep. I told you, I'm the only one that can keep you safe and get you dope. She don't know the Valley Boys. How's she gonna keep you safe? Huh? I gave you everything, you traitor!"

"Oh, for the love of God, shut up." Duke tore off another piece of duct tape and slapped it over Emory's mouth, making sure to make good contact with his nose. Emory squealed in muffled pain and fell over again. Tears began to leak from his eyes.

"Ya'll go on ahead," Jane said to Duke. "We got things under control here."

Duke whistled at Nukem. "You keep an eye on him, okay?"

Nuke trotted over to Emory and sat down in front of him. Emory shrank back away from him. Duke gave his sister a sarcastic little salute before climbing back into his saddle. He motioned for Leonard to lead the way. Once they were gone, Willa pulled Emory back up to a sitting position.

"I'm done dealing with your shit." Jane squatted down in front of him. "Just so you know, I just so happen to know that you are a lying sack of crap. The three of us are actual members of the Blue Valley Boys. I know for a fact that you are some shady little prick, poaching passage fees from the Valley Boys from this intersection. Why there aren't any actual Valley Boys here right now is baffling, but I fully intend on making sure that lapse is rectified."

Emory protested in muffled yells and inarticulate mumbling. Jane ripped off the tape.

"How do you know I ain't one of them, huh? How do I know you ain't the ones lyin' to me?"

Jane and Willa held up their arms to reveal identical tattoos: two simple, overlapping triangles, the symbol of the Blue Valley Boys. They each also had a tattoo on the inside of their arms, just below the elbow. Jane had the Roman numeral I; Willa had the numeral II. It was safe to assume Duke had the numeral III.

Emory's eyes widened in silent panic. He hung his head and began to cry. Of all people he had tried to rob, he held up three actual members of the Valley Boys.

"Like I said, we won't kill you. But you are poaching on Blue Valley territory, and as a good, upstanding member of the Valley Boys, I am obligated to turn you in. We won't kill you, but I can't say the same for them."

"You ain't obligated to shit, man!" Emory pleaded. "You ain't gotta tell nobody we was even here. Just let me go and I swear I won't ever come back. Please."

"On the contrary," Jane said calmly. She stood up and looked down at him. "We tried to be nice. We offered you the bobcat, which was enough to pay the passage of at least six people, by the way. You brought this on yourself." Jane turned to Willa. "You got this?"

Willa nodded. "Yeah. I got this. You go do your thing."

With that, the strong confident façade disappeared from Jane's face. She turned and ran to hide behind a concrete barricade on the side of the road. Willa could hear the retching and splattering of the reappearance of Jane's breakfast. A stifled sob, a few shuddering breaths, then right back into retching. Willa sighed as she soaked a rag in water from her canteen and took them to her sister. A quiet conversation between a soft, concerned voice and a quivering, weak one. Willa reappeared from behind the barricade.

"What's wrong with her? She sick?" Emory asked, cautiously curious.

If looks could kill, Willa's would've melted the skin right off his face. She picked up Emory's revolver and opened the chamber. It wasn't even loaded.

"Anxiety," she closed the revolver with a snap and tucked it into the back of her belt. "Any kind of confrontation wreaks havoc on her."

Emory was genuinely confused. "She didn't seem so anxious a few minutes ago. She was downright scary!"

"Yeah, well, it's called putting on a brave face, and she's a master at it." There was a strange mix of sadness and pride in her voice.

Duke and Leonard returned not long after. There wasn't much of value—a couple of kitchen knives, a tent, a cook pot, and three cans of green beans. There was also a quart of moonshine, but no drugs. Emory saw what he had assumed before. Duke did indeed round out the set of tattoos, the double triangles on his wrist and numeral III beneath his elbow.

Willa checked on Jane again. Jane came around from behind the barrier. She cast a disgusted look at Emory before climbing back into the saddle. Willa pulled Emory to his feet and they made their way into what used to be Dillsboro, North Carolina.

Just beyond the barricaded intersection, the town of Dillsboro opened up before them. It was a tiny little riverfront town, filled with little shops and quaint little inns with boarded up windows. The once pristine white houses were now faded and sagging. The city limits were marked by a sign, a large piece of plywood with crudely painted, bright blue letters that read:

Blue Valley Boys territory. Do not take that which is not freely given.

"I saw that when we came in. What does that even mean?" Emory asked.

"It means don't steal," Willa snapped.

Jane gave a little more thorough reply. "It's the only real law that the Valley Boys follow and enforce. If it belongs to someone else, and they do not willingly give it to you, do not take it from them."

"It applies to more than just material things. It means anything, like permission to collect passage fees," Duke said.

"Or sexual consent." Willa kicked Emory in the back of the head.

"So you're down on two counts."

"If you were really a member of the Valley Boys, you would've known that."

"And wouldn't have tried to rob us in the first place."

Emory looked like he would be sick.

"What will they do to us?" Leonard asked.

"Well, I'll see what strings I can pull for you since you didn't really do anything but trust the wrong person," Jane said.

"Emory on the other hand," Duke said. "Well, at least he'll still have his other hand. And hey..." He snapped his fingers as if he had a sudden thought. "If you're lucky, you might get to keep the hand you jerk with."

Jane, Duke, and Willa laughed. Leonard giggled. Emory vomited.

Chapter Three

There wasn't much to speak of in Dillsboro, abandoned buildings, overgrown lawns, weeds poking through the cracks in the asphalt. There wasn't a soul to be seen. Dark windows stared out of store fronts like the empty eyes of skulls. Plants fought each other for dominance in what used to be meticulously manicured medians. The air was cleaner, the flowers were brighter, the birds sang louder. The world was much better off without man trying to tame it.

Duke started to whistle *The Twilight Zone* theme song.

"Will you cut it out?" Willa whispered. The eerie atmosphere felt like a slumbering spirit that they didn't want to disturb.

Nuke wandered off to sniff around a clump of bushes. He flushed out a squirrel and merrily chased it across the street. The squirrel darted up a tree and chattered angrily at Nuke, who stood with his paws on the trunk barking at it.

"Do you think we ought to have a poke around?" Duke asked.

"Why? The Valley Boys will have cleaned it all out ages ago," Willa replied.

Jane stopped Mahz in front of a faded yellow house and slid down from the saddle. The house sat on a small hill so close to the road the yard was held back by a stone retaining wall.

"Might as well," Jane said. "We'll just hit a few places and if we don't turn up much, we'll keep going." She led Mahz up the steep driveway and secured the reins to the porch railing.

Willa climbed down from her saddle and pushed Emory toward

the empty house and cuffed him to the porch railing. "You stay here while we go have a look around."

"You're just gonna leave me here?" Emory cried.

"You'd prefer we take you to the Valley Boys first?" Duke said, raising an eyebrow. Emory sat down on the steps and wrapped his arm around the railing.

"I'll stay and keep an eye on him," Jane volunteered. "I need to sit down for a bit anyway."

"You sure?" Willa wasn't too keen on the idea.

"Yeah. I'm good. Ya'll need to hurry though. It'll be dark soon."

Duke whistled at Nuke. "You stay here and keep an eye on him, 'kay?"

Nuke trotted over to Emory and sat in front of him. Emory shrank back against the steps.

Willa, Duke, and Leonard walked across the street to the little shopping center. The building only housed four stores so it wouldn't take long to go through it.

"How come you don't carry a gun like they do?"

Jane deliberately ignored him and dug through Mahz's saddle bag. There was a good reason why she didn't carry a gun, but she wasn't about to tell him.

"Hey. I'm talking to you."

Jane pulled out a toothbrush and a small glass jar of powdered toothpaste. She took a swig of water and scooped up some of the powder with the brush. She brushed her teeth while Emory continued his attempts to talk to her.

"How can someone as scared as you be such a bitch?"

Jane spat on the ground. "The same way somebody as ugly as you can be such a douchebag."

Jane walked past him and across the porch of the little house. It was a quaint little cottage. Each of the front windows had a wooden flower box full of the dried brown husks of long forgotten annuals. The porch wrapped around the left side of the house to the back.

She walked around the house, peeking in the windows and into the neighboring yards. On the back deck, faded blue curtains sighed in the broken kitchen window, reaching out to her as she passed. How long had it been since someone had been inside this house? Since someone cooked in the kitchen? Bandaged a scuffed knee in the bathroom? Fished a teddy bear from under the bed?

Jane came back around and opened the front door. It creaked in protest. Her boots left footprints in dust that now coated a long couch that stood in front of a cobwebbed fireplace. Dust that had settled on the rug between them and the Legos scattered across it. Dust that had lain undisturbed for nearly four years. Four years since the country was attacked, civilization fell, and life as they knew it had come to a screeching halt.

America had fallen victim to her own hubris. After centuries of throwing her weight around and meddling in the affairs of everyone else, the world had finally had enough. At least, America's enemies had. The threat of nuclear war had become a reality when Russia decided that "the enemy of my enemy is my friend." It wasn't even really a war. Caught completely off guard, America had been attacked on both sides. They'd targeted major cities, killing millions of innocent people; but more devastatingly, they'd targeted the power grid. Everything they had taken for granted, everything that had made the world modern, was gone.

Jane sneezed. Despite the dust and the musty smell of abandoned hope, they could stay here for the night if they had to.

Meanwhile, Willa, Duke, and Leonard were sifting through the scattered remains of a thrift shop. Willa flipped through the already picked over racks of clothing, while Duke and Leonard sifted through the piles of shoes, housewares, and toys that had been left on the floor. Leonard, trying to be helpful, picked up a wall thermometer and showed it to Duke.

"Hey, what about this?"

Duke looked at it. "Nah, man. It's busted. It needs to be re-calibrated, see? It only reads in Celsius." He ran his fingers through his hair.

Leonard looked at Duke, looked at the thermometer, then shrugged and threw it back on the pile.

"You are such an ass." Willa kept her voice low as Leonard picked through another pile on the other side of the room.

"But he makes it so easy," Duke sniggered.

Willa tossed her head back and rolled her eyes. It was only then did she notice a large air vent on the wall near the ceiling just above a tall display shelf.

"Give me a lift."

"Oh, sure. I'll just lift a 190 pound woman up over my head with one hand. No problem."

She was so used to having Duke around as muscle, she'd forgotten about his shoulder.

"Okay, then just make sure I don't fall." She grabbed the shelf and began to scale the wobbly display.

"Oh, so I don't have to lift the 190 pound woman one-handed. I just have to catch her when she falls. Fantastic."

"I am not 190 pounds."

"You are every bit of 190 pounds and every bit of it muscle. I have lifted your skinny ass many times, and you are not nearly as light as you look."

"Oh, bite me."

"Nah. You're too lean. Good meat has a lot of fat. Melts into the meat and—"

"Will you shut up and pay attention? Toss me your multi-tool." She perched on top of the display in front of the vent.

"Why?" he asked, looking up at her.

"Because I need it."

"Don't you think you shoulda thought of that before you

climbed up there?"

"Seriously, dude. Just let me see it."

"Are you going to give it back?"

"DUKE!"

Duke laughed. "Okay. Okay. Here." He pulled the tool off of his belt and tossed it up to her.

Willa unscrewed the vent cover and pulled it away. "Ah-HA!" There was a six pack of toilet paper and a box of tampons hidden inside. She tossed it down.

"Anything else?" Leonard had joined Duke looking up at Willa.

"No, but if they hid that, I'm sure they hid something else around here."

As they walked out, a pile of dolls near the front door caught her attention. They were the soft body type, with plastic arms, legs, and heads. But the way they were laying on each other didn't look quite right. Like their bodies were heavier than the cotton they were filled with. She picked one up.

"I'd have thought you'd outgrown dolls by now."

"Shut up."

Sure enough, the doll was much heavier than it should have been. She flicked open her pocket knife and slit open the back of the doll. A handful of AAA batteries fell into her hand.

"Oh shit!" Duke picked up another doll and handed it to Leonard. "Open it, dude."

Leonard sliced open the doll with a cheap pocket knife he found. More batteries. AA this time. They opened the remaining dolls and ended up with a small horde.

Duke shook his head. "It amazes me how you manage to find stuff like that. A true Hufflepuff, indeed."

"Shut up." Willa tried to sound aggravated, but there was a soft edge of amusement and pride in her voice.

Willa walked outside.

"Hold up. Come back," Duke said.

She went back inside and Duke pointed at a bathroom scale by the door. Willa scowled at him, but stood on it, 182.

Leonard trailed behind as they walked back to Jane and Emory. Jane stood to greet them. "Find anything?"

"Toilet paper, tampons, and a small gold mine of batteries."

"Awesome. We can tell Nolan what we found, let them do another search later. What time is it?"

"A little after one."

"Good. We've got plenty of time. We're only about two miles from the courthouse. We'll be there in about an hour or so. We need to get there before dark. The last thing we want to do is sneak up on Nolan at night."

"I never thought I'd say this," Duke said, "but I can't wait to see that cranky old bastard again."

Chapter Four

Halfway to Sylva, they were stopped by a gang of what could only be called rednecks. There were three of them in various combinations of Wranglers, t-shirts, ball caps and boots. They were about their age. One had dark hair and rich, russet skin. The other two were identical twin blonds.

They stopped between a derelict brewery and a U-Haul rental place. The road had been newly paved just before everything fell, so the white and yellow lines were still sharp against the smooth dark black asphalt. The tarmac reflected what heat it had absorbed, while a cool breeze danced through the air. The siblings raised their arms to show their triangle tattoos. The Guard returned the gesture.

"You're unfamiliar. Identify yourselves," the dark-haired man said. They pulled out their old driver's licenses. Nuke walked up to the Guards and put his head in their hands while they looked over their licenses. The Guards took turns petting him and rubbing his ears.

"I'm from Cashiers Village. This is my brother and sister, from Oconee. We're just passing through," Jane said.

"I'm José. This is Josh and Chris." He reached up and shook their hands.

"We found these two poaching the highway cross point. We're turning them in."

The Guards looked at each other in confusion, then one of the blonds spoke. "They're not one of us."

Jane rolled her eyes. "Yes, I am aware of that. That's why we brought them in."

"Where are the Guards that were supposed to be there?"

"No idea. They weren't there when we came through. Just these two. That might be something you want to look into."

The twins giggled.

"I bet I know where they are," Josh said.

Garcia cursed under his breath. "Son of a bitch. Alright, go on through. We'll get it straightened out."

The atmosphere changed as they left Dillsboro and got closer to Sylva. They started to see more people along the road. There were lots of children playing in the yards of the houses they passed. One boy chased another across the street and tackled him. They wrestled until their mother came out and broke them up. A burly looking woman held clothes pins between her teeth as she hung laundry out on the line to dry. She waved at them as they passed before swatting at the two boys that were now pulling her laundry down. A couple of older men argued over the engine of a large Ford truck. They didn't smile, but they did wave in acknowledgment. Blue Valley was a rough town, but they welcomed strangers with open arms.

They approached the back of an impressive white courthouse around two in the afternoon. The iconic courthouse was the centerpiece of downtown Sylva, an imposing building situated at the top of a hill at the end of Main Street. Having been once turned from courthouse to public library, it had since been turned from library into the main headquarters for the Blue Valley Boys.

A small group of people were gathered near the atrium door. Most of them were men, but there were a few women chatting amongst themselves. The babble of conversation died as the group approached. Apparently, this was supposed to be a private meeting, because some of the people looked confused that they were being interrupted. One of them approached Willa.

"Just who the hell are you?" he demanded. He looked like the kind of man who thought very highly of himself and assumed everybody else did, too. Willa finally started to feel irritated. "That is the third time today someone has demanded to know who we are. I'm Willa Campbell. How does the knowledge of my name help you in any way?"

"Don't you get an attitude with me, bitch." The man grabbed her arm.

"Hey, asshole! Let me go." Willa writhed and twisted, but he maintained his iron grip on her bicep.

"Don't you start shit with me, bitch. I am not in the mood." Willa spat in his face. The man snarled and raised his hand.

A man approached him and pulled him back. "Let her go, Troy."

He looked strikingly similar to Troy, but his beard was neatly trimmed and he wore glasses. Troy pushed the man.

"Back off, Rhys!"

Duke took a single step forward, his arms crossed. The look in his eyes dared the man to swing at his sister. Nuke raised his hackles. Before anyone could do anything, a loud, heavily accented voice came from near the building.

"Who the hell is yelling oot here?" A wild-looking man came around the corner yelling in a heavy Scottish accent. His white hair stood on end, and there was a crazed expression in his eyes. He resembled a demented Doc Emmett Brown from *Back to the Future*, if he had been wearing anything more than a tartan kilt and cowboy boots. He walked with a twisting limp and leaned on a heavy, knobby walking stick.

"It's us, you Celtic dick, now call off your hound," Willa cried.

"Who the hell yeh think yeh are, yeh bampot! I swear to God, I'll—" He pushed past the crowd and finally saw who he was talking to. He crossed himself. "Sweet Mary n' Joseph. Troy, let her go."

The man released Willa. She rubbed her arm and glared at him.

Troy looked at the Scottish man in disbelief. "You know these people, Nolan?" he barked.

Rhys shoved him. "Can you be civil for once in your life?"

Nolan ignored Troy and cupped Willa's face in his free hand.

"Willa Campbell. Ah've missed you, lass."

"Thanks, Nolan," Willa said. She hugged him. Over his shoulder, she flipped Troy the bird.

Nolan hugged Jane. "Ah never thought ah'd see you again."

"Good to see you too, Nolan." Jane couldn't help but grin.

He noticed Duke standing behind Jane. He shook Duke's hand. "Good tae see ya lad."

"Who are these people, Nolan?" Rhys asked.

"This is Jane, an old friend o' mine, and her brother n' sister. Ah've known Jane for a very long time." He gave Troy a warning look. "But all three o' them are important tae me. Ah'm very glad tae see them alive."

He noticed Leonard and Emory. "Who are they?"

"This is Leonard, and that one is Emory. We came across them poaching passage tolls at the 441 intersection," Jane said.

"By 'they,' she means Emory, and by 'poaching,' she means mugging innocent people," Willa added.

Jane put a hand on Leonard's shoulder. "Leonard's only crime was trusting the wrong person. Don't be too hard on him. You can give his punishment to Emory on top of his own, and it still wouldn't be enough."

She gave Leonard a reassuring smile.

"He tried tae mug you?" Nolan asked Jane as he approached Emory.

"Oh, no. He thought he was, but he never got the opportunity," Duke replied smugly.

"He also thought he was gonna get a pass at me and Jane," Willa sneered.

Nolan approached Emory. Emory flinched back. Nolan grabbed his chin and turned his face so he could see his broken nose in the light.

"I suppose this is yer handiwork, Willa?"

"Yup."

Nolan glared at Emory, "You tried tae rob ma friends?"

"They're lyin'! I swear to God, I—"

"You tried tae rape them?"

"I done told you. They're lyin'."

Nolan jabbed him in the ribs with his staff. Emory fell to his knees, struggling to pull ragged breaths.

Nolan turned to two of the men gathered. "Give Leonard a room at the tavern, make sure he's comfortable. Tomorrow, take him tae Chuck a' the Campus. Lock this one up. We'll deal with him in the morning."

One of them grabbed Emory and frog marched him away. The other clapped Leonard on the shoulder and began talking to him about the tavern and his accommodations there.

Nolan turned back to Jane. "We have gathered for oor quarterly meeting o' the minds. Tonight, there will be dinner n' discussion. We were not expecting more people, but it should be easy enough tae add three more places. Please, stay as ma guest. Your siblings as well."

"We would be honored and grateful, Nolan." Jane turned to Willa and gestured her forward. Willa came forward, leading Jack. Jane reached up and pointed to the deer on the top of the pack. "A gesture of our gratitude."

Two more of the men came forward and pulled down the deer. Nolan inspected it and gave it his approval.

"Rhys, go tell the staff that we have three unexpected guests. Have them prepare rooms for them n' set them a place a' oor dinner table tonight. Troy, take their horses to the stables. See to it they're well cared for," Nolan said.

The man who had accosted Willa upon their arrival turned to her and gave her an evil look. He took their reins and disappeared to follow Nolan's orders. Nuke looked up at Duke, then followed Troy and the horses. Nolan led them through the atrium. Their footsteps echoed in the empty space.

"Dinnae pay him no mind. He's just crabbit."

Duke leaned over and whispered to Jane, "I can't tell if he's speaking English or not."

Jane translated. "Don't pay attention to Troy. He's just in a pissy mood."

"Yeh'll be staying in the motel below on Main Street. But for now, you can make yerselves at hame here." He pointed to a door on the right. "Through there is the meeting rooms n' ma office. Oh, manners! This is ma assistant, Rhys. You had the pleasure of meeting his brother Troy."

Rhys shook their hands. "I'm sorry about my brother. He can be a bit of a hot head."

Willa raised her eyebrows. "A bit?"

"Oh, like you've got room to talk," Duke said.

They followed Nolan through the double doors on the left. The many aisles of shelves of books were still in place. Jane walked slowly down one of the aisles, running her fingers across the spines of the books. She inhaled deeply, relishing in the soft almondy scent of the old books. She sneezed from the dust.

Willa sank wearily into chair. She laid her head back and closed her eyes. Nolan sat with them, laying his walking stick against the arm of his chair. Rhys remained standing, keeping an eye on the door. Duke settled gently into another. He pressed his hand against his shoulder and grimaced.

He looked at Duke. "Ah can have someone look a' that shoulder o' yers if yeh like."

"If you don't mind. It is starting to ache a little. Nothing I can't handle, but all the same…"

Troy returned. He cast a murderous glare at the Campbells.

"Oh good. Yer back. Can yeh go fetch the doctor, please? Duke needs some attention."

"Duke always needs attention," Willa said without opening her eyes. "He feeds on it."

"I no longer rely on mortal food like you peasants. I subsist on the admiration of others." He grinned like the Cheshire Cat.

"Good. I hope you starve to death."

"Thanks to denial, I'm immortal."

Nolan and Jane laughed. Troy's temple twitched. Willa rolled her head to look at Duke in incredulity.

"You are such a child."

"I know you are, but what am I?"

Willa rolled her eyes and stuck her tongue out at him. He stuck his out at her.

"Oh for Pete's sake," Jane laughed. "Both of you are actual five-year-olds."

Troy glared at Nolan. "I am not your errand boy, Nolan."

Rhys rubbed the bridge of his nose, pushing his glasses up on his forehead. "For God's sake Troy…"

"Ah never said yeh were. Yeh need tae check yer tone wi' me, lad," Nolan warned.

"Me? Check my tone? These three just show up out of nowhere. Grown adults that act like children. You're the only one who knows who they are. And you invite them in, treating them like honored guests? What the hell is wrong with you, Nolan?"

Willa looked up. "Listen here you prick."

Troy rounded on her. "Don't you start your shit with me again. I won't back down again."

Duke stood up and squared up to Troy. Rhys moved to stand between them, holding up his hands to keep them apart. Jane peered nervously around the aisle.

"The only thing wrong wi' me is tha' ah continue tae put up wi' yer shite, Troy," Nolan growled. "Yeh need tae calm down. Go fetch the doctor, then have yerself a drink. Ah understand this is a stressful time, but these are old friends o' mine, n' they deserve yer respect, just like all o' the others gathering here this weekend. Yeh need tae back off n' go."

Troy didn't say anything during his dressing down. He turned on his heel and stormed back out of the room.

"What the hell is his problem?" Willa asked.

"He's a bawbag, tha's his problem," Nolan said. "We're having a meeting wi' the deputies. Organizing this meeting always gets his panties in a wad."

"Deputies? You have a police force?"

"Not quite that kind of deputy. Our territory continues tae expand every year. It's getting harder n' harder for me tae keep track o' who lives within oor borders, where the borders are, all tha'. There's not enough people tae need mayors or anything, but ah have people that live in n' watch over certain areas o' oor territory. They help me govern by proxy. We have a little get-together four times a year tae regroup."

"That sounds a lot like how the Vikings did things," Duke said.

"Yes, well, their model seemed the best fit for us for now."

Troy didn't return, but a gray-haired woman in a flowing brown skirt came through the door to the atrium.

"Oh, good. Duke, Willa, Jane, this is Gloria. She's our resident doctor."

"I keep telling you, Nolan. I am not a doctor. You need to find a real one to tend to this town."

"I know, I know. But in the meantime, my friend here needs yeh tae take a look a' him."

Duke scooted forward in his seat and sat up straighter as Gloria unwound the bandages.

"Who bound you up?"

Duke nodded at Willa. "My sister. Said I couldn't be trusted not to move, so she tied me down."

"Good thinking." Gloria tugged at the t-shirt bandages covering the stitches, but it was glued to the wound with dried blood and pus. "That's not a good sign. I'll have to soak it, loosen it up so I can pull it off. Would you mind coming with me to my office? I promise you'll be back in time for dinner."

Duke stood and followed her back through the atrium. Nolan turned to the sisters. "Yer're welcome tae stay here n' rest until dinner. If yeh will excuse me, ah have some business tae attend tae. Dinner will be upstairs in the conference room a' six. Ah look forward tae finding oot what has brought yeh back tae oor little corner o' the world."

Nolan and Rhys left them in the library and went upstairs. Jane looked at Willa. "Well? What do you think?"

"I think Nolan is still the same ornery old bastard he always was, but his right-hand man is a dick."

"Yeah, things seem a little tense around here."

"You can say that again. How long do you think we'll stay here?"

"Just the night, probably. We need to get to the Village as soon as possible." Jane thought about Duke and how he complained of pain. He had brushed it off in his overtly manly way, but Jane knew better than to take it at face value.

At six, they entered the conference room where the long table had been set for dinner. Nolan took his place at the head of the table. Jane and Willa joined him, taking the two places on his left. Rhys returned and began to take his seat on Nolan's right.

"Move down a seat, Rhys," Nolan said, "Ah'll have ma guest sit next to me, if yeh dinnae mind."

Duke grinned at Rhys and took his seat. The other guests filled the remaining seats. There was an impressive spread of meats and vegetables before them. Roasted corn, potatoes, and beans sat alongside rabbit, chicken, and deer. Beef had become rather scarce in recent years.

Nolan stood. "Thank yeh all for being here tonight. This is our fourth n' final meeting o' the Blue Valley Boys o' the year. We will be discussing borders, populations, n' other diplomatic stuff. But for the moment, please, eat, drink, n' enjoy yerselves."

He sat back down and pulled the nearest plate of potatoes

toward him. The rest of the guests, waiting for their fearless leader to begin, began helping themselves to the feast.

"So," Nolan said as he ladled a generous helping of potatoes onto his plate, "what brings yeh back tae oor little corner o' hell?"

Duke spoke around a mouthful of food, pointing to his shoulder. "I got into a little scuffle."

Willa rolled her eyes. "He damned near got his arm ripped off."

"We're going to get him checked out at the medical center in the Village," Jane replied.

"Ah, well, yeh'll have tae wait then. Part o' the road got washed oot, couple miles past the Campus. Ah've got some guys working on it, but it'll be a few days, at least."

"Are you serious? What happened?"

"We had a mighty storm blow through last week. Hurricane season, yeh know. Tha' plus the fact that we haven't had any road maintenance in, what? Three years now? Four? Ah lose track." He wiped his mouth with a linen napkin. "In the meantime, the three o' yeh will be ma guests. Until the road is fixed, make yerselves at home."

"Thank you, Nolan. We'll do what we can to earn our keep," Willa said.

He waved her offer away. "Nonsense. From the look o' it, yeh've spent the last year doing naught but surviving. I want yeh tae relax, tae enjoy yoerselves!"

Once the meal was finished, many of the guests thanked Nolan for his hospitality and left to find a bed. The Campbells, along with Rhys, followed Nolan into a small room on the second floor. There was a pair of leather chairs by the large plate glass windows that overlooked the perpetually darkened Main Street. In the center of the room was a small but heavy round table surrounded by six chairs. On the table were a pack of cards, an ashtray, a box of matches, and a pack of cigarettes.

Rhys lit the gas lamp in the middle of the table. Nolan motioned for them to sit at the table, and offered each of them a cigarette. Duke politely refused his, but Jane and Willa were grateful. They had smoked the last of their stale cigarettes two weeks ago.

Rhys turned to Willa. "I want to apologize for my brother's behavior earlier. We've all been a little on edge lately. Since it's starting to get cold, we've had more and more people coming in, stealing supplies, threatening our people. It gets worse and worse every year. That, plus helping Nolan organize this thing with meeting with the deputies, we're just stretched a little thin." He looked more than stretched thin. The shadows under his eyes belied his powerful posture. The poor man was exhausted.

"No worries." She patted him on the arm. "I understand." She gave him a sweet smile. "But if he does that shit again, I will hand him his teeth in a jar."

"I don't doubt that one little bit." He laughed. He touched her arm gingerly. In the soft light of the gas lamp, he could see long purple bruises, the same size as his fingers, beginning to blossom on her arm.

"Quit flirting, Rhys, n' deal." Nolan slid the pack of cards across the table to him. He walked across the room to a side table with an array of short glasses and several glass bottles.

Duke and Jane purposefully took the two chairs on Nolan's left, leaving Willa to sit next to Rhys. Willa glared at them.

"What're we playing?" Duke asked.

"Poker." Rhys slid a pair of cards to each of them.

Nolan passed out glasses and filled each of them with a measure of stout brown liquor.

"Rhys n' ah spend many nights playing cards. Yeh remember what ah taught yeh?" he asked Jane.

"Of course, I do. We've spent most nights playing as well."

"Three years of perfecting the craft. Not much else to do since the wi-fi's been down." Duke glanced at his cards.

"I'm impressed with what you've done with this place,

Nolan," Jane said.

"Well, ah haven't done much. Other than converting this room intae a study, n' fixin' up th' offices for Rhys n' mahself, ah haven't really changed anything."

"That's what I'm impressed about. The stacks are exactly where they've always been. It's nice to see you've made an effort to preserve the collection."

"Well, it wasn't much o' a conscious decision, as much as it was laziness. But knowing that someone appreciates it, ah'll see tae it that we dae more than just live amongst it."

"That would be a great thing to see. Reading is one of the few past times we have left to enjoy that doesn't require electricity," Jane said.

Willa pulled a cigarette out of the pack Nolan gave her and lit it. "Oh wow. This is fresh." She was surprised.

"Courtesy o' our friends down a' the Campus," Nolan replied.

"What's the Campus?" Jane lit one of her own.

Nolan settled himself into his seat and looked at his cards. "The old Western Carolina University campus. Some o' our people have settled there n' turned it intae a farm."

"I thought the university was abandoned?"

"It was up until aboot two years ago. Some o' our people saw the advantage o' those large athletic fields. They've been running it ever since."

"Is that where the vegetables from dinner came from?"

Rhys gave a raspy, coughing laugh. "Not quite that kind of farm."

"They're more o' a, uh, pharmaceutical farm," Nolan explained.

Willa's eyes widened. "It's a drug farm?"

"It's all organic." Rhys reached forward and tapped his cigarette over the ashtray. "There's no meth or heroin or anything like that."

"So just pot?"

"Tha' n' mushrooms. They do have some crops; corn, wheat, barley, stuff like tha'. They use it tae make beer n' liquor. It's part o' the reason we're having troubles wi' the National Guard in

Cashiers Village."

"The Campus has been growing exponentially over the past year. People come from all over to trade, which brings business to us," Rhys explained.

"How is that a problem? That would bring more business to the Village, too, wouldn't it?" Willa asked.

"It would, and does. But they don't seem to be satisfied with working with us. They want control of the Campus, and by extension, us." Rhys flipped over the next five cards.

Jane had other concerns. "Wait, hold up. Did you say the National Guard? What does the National Guard have to do with any of this?"

"Well, it seems that government has set up shop in the Village." Nolan lit a cigarette. "It looks like yer old friends have made some new ones in yer absence."

"That's great, isn't it?"

"Yeh would think so, but ah'm not so sure. We used tae be on decent terms with the Village. Live n' let live. A little trade here n' there. But all tha' has stopped. Gotten worse in fact. All the lads we used tae deal wi' on the border are gone. Replaced with 'trained professionals,'" Nolan sneered. "A bunch o' wankstains is what they are."

Willa snorted in her drink and coughed. Rhys pounded her on the back. Jane looked wary.

"What do you mean by that?"

"Hostile. Think they're all mighty n' important. One ah saw hasn't barely heard his voice drop. A buncha kids wi' guns n' an overinflated sense o' self importance."

Jane looked at him in confusion. "And you're scared of a pack of teenagers?"

"It's not them. It's the ones tha' put them there. They answer tae somebody. Somebody has given them uniforms n' guns n' told them that we're the enemy."

Jane was beginning to understand what he meant. She remembered the small governing body that had formed in Cashiers Village before she left. It was more of a council, all local guys that held respect in the community. There was Jim, who ran the large automotive service center; Larry Joseph, ran the only hardware store in town; Robert Lowe had been a municipal judge; Don Stephenson from the Chamber of Commerce; and Charlie Mack, owner of the largest Christmas tree farm in the tri-county area. Jane knew in her heart that not one of them would have placed anyone, especially teenagers, in a position that would harm the fragile alliance the Village had with the Blue Valley Boys, much less in a position that might lead them to harm.

"And you said the National Guard is doing this?" Jane asked.

"From what ah understand. Or at least, tha's what they're calling themselves."

"So what exactly is your major concern, Nolan?" Duke leaned forward.

"To be honest, ah'm not exactly sure. Ah'm not even totally sure who 'they' are. They haven't really done anything yet, except for ending oor trade agreement. All ah know is, ah have a bad feeling aboot them. I dinnae like them, whoever they are."

Chapter Five

Despite Nolan's insistence that they relax and enjoy their stay in Blue Valley, they found it difficult to remain idle for too long. Jane still hadn't fully recovered from her anxiety attack the day before, but Willa and Duke flourished in their new environments.

Having spent the last six months in the sole company of his sisters, Duke was overjoyed to be in the midst of other men, not to mention women he wasn't related to. He fell into a group of men splitting wood for the coming winter. He fumbled at first, having only one good arm. Gloria had done an excellent job cleaning him up. It had renewed his vigor, even if it was temporary. Eventually he found a rhythm and had no problem swinging an axe one handed. He tired quickly though and had to settle for stacking wood as the other guys split it.

Willa was right at home behind the bar at the tavern, making new friends and drinking the men under the table. One of her regulars was Rhys. He insisted that he frequented the tavern long before Willa came to town, but Jane and Duke teased her relentlessly anyway.

The longer Jane stayed in Blue Valley, the more anxious she was to get to the Village. She stood on the front balcony of the courthouse, looking out at the mountains on the horizon. Just on the other side of those mountains was Cashiers Village. After hearing Nolan's account, her mind raced with wild and increasingly improbable ideas of what had befallen the town she had grown to love. Her heart yearned to see her old home, but her apprehensive mind remembered why she left in the first place. Haunted by painful memories, she swore she'd never go back. But here she was, just a handful of miles away, at the foot of the mountain, staring out at the hazy blue ripple across the horizon.

While Duke and Willa socialized and made themselves at home with the residents of Blue Valley, Jane chose to stick close to Nolan. Her anxiety attacks always left her feeling vulnerable for at least a couple of days afterward. She looked forward to a few quiet days, hanging out with Nolan, listening and watching him rule his little kingdom, and perusing the library.

The first day after their arrival, Nolan held a sort of court, listening to complaints and accusations from the people he ruled over and making judgments. There were several rows of folding stadium seats facing a wide blank wall flanked by two doors. He sat in an impressive armed chair facing the seats, his hand wrapped around his staff. He was wearing his kilt and boots again, but mercifully added a faded black Pink Floyd band shirt. Rhys sat on his right side with a clipboard, taking notes on the proceedings. There were a dozen or so other Blue Valley citizens making up the audience. Jane sat on the far end of the front row.

The first was a grievance between two neighboring men.

"State yer names." Nolan put his chin in his hand, resting his elbow on the arm of his chair, and sighed.

"James Greaves." He was tall and gangly. There were bags under his eyes and deep wrinkles around the corners of his mouth. He clutched a frayed leather hat in front of him with his long bony fingers.

"Vance Hoggart." The second man was short, fat, and endlessly arrogant.

"What brings yeh back 'ere today?" Nolan's expression was droll and completely uninterested.

"Mr. Greaves has stolen one of my pigs, and I demand compensation!" Hoggart huffed.

Nolan rolled his eyes. "What evidence dae yoeh have tae prove yer case?"

"One of my pigs is missing, and there's footprints in the mud leading in the direction of his house."

"N' there's no possible way those footprints are yer oon?" Nolan's sarcasm went right over Hoggart's head.

"Of course not. What use would I have going to his house?" Hoggart was offended.

James raised his hand. Nolan turned slightly to look at him without picking up his chin. "Yeh have a rebuttal, Mr. Greaves?"

"Yes, sir. Mr. Hoggart did come to my house. Two days prior, to complain about my dog—"

"That flea-infested mongrel has been sniffing around my back door." Hoggart quivered in outrage. His face flushed red, and he began to sweat profusely. He pulled out a yellowed handkerchief and mopped his brow.

Greaves turned to him and argued, "Only because you throw your damned grease and gristle out the kitchen window." He looked back at Nolan. "I did not steal his damned pig."

"N' yer evidence for yer claim?"

"He was plastered drunk when he accosted me about my dog. He went home and slaughtered that pig hisself. He just don't remember it."

"Where is the pig now?"

"Gone!" Hoggart bellowed. "This son of a bitch stole my pig and hid it somewhere if he ain't butchered it already."

Nolan looked at James.

"Coyotes, I'd guess."

"So neither o' yeh have any actual evidence against th' other."

"I said I did, didn't I? I got his footprints in the mud around my pen."

"And yet we have Mr. Greaves' account that they are yer drunken footprints." Nolan turned to Jane, "What dae yeh think?"

"Me?"

"Yes, yeh. What dae yeh think?"

Jane was surprised that he would ask her opinion. She stumbled a moment before saying, "Well, I'd give him the benefit of the doubt. Innocent until proven guilty. Neither of them have any proof, so neither of them get a judgment."

"Well put." Nolan nodded. He turned back to the two men. "Both o' yer have been a pain in ma arse more than once, usually at the same time. I'm tired o' both o' yeh. Yer both ignorant arsewipes wi' nothing better tae dae than bicker like wet hens. Ah'm sick o' yeh wasting ma time. Both o' yeh get out. Ah'm not making any more judgments for either o' yeh."

Next was a young couple found squatting in a house on the outer edges of Nolan's territory. Both of them were as dark as rich mahogany. The woman's hair was wrapped in a beautiful scarf that was tied at the crown. They stood in front of Nolan's chair, trembling, clutching each other's hand. Jane couldn't blame them. Nolan's guys flanked his chair, and they were pretty intimidating. Nolan leaned forward, elbows on his knees, staff in both hands.

"What's yer name, lad?"

"Drake, and this is my wife, Deandra." He did his best to appear calm, but his voice shook. "Please, sir, we didn't realize we were trespassing. It was an honest mistake. I—"

Nolan held up his hand. His voice was relaxed and reassuring, vastly different than it was dealing with the pig thieves.

"It's all right, lad. Yer not in trouble." The tension in their eyes eased away, but they still regarded Nolan warily. "Ah understand that oor borders can be ambiguous, especially in the more remote areas. Let me be the first tae formally welcome yeh. Welcome tae Blue Valley. Ma name is Nolan. Ah run things around here."

Deandra looked up at Jane, who smiled. She looked back at Nolan. "Thank you, sir."

"So, are you, like, the king or something?" Drake asked.

"If yeh want tae call me tha', ah'll not stop yeh. But this isn't so much a kingdom, as it is a, uh..." He looked at Jane, searching for the right word.

"It's more of a loose coalition of like-minded people," Jane supplied.

"Precisely," Nolan said.

Drake looked back at Jane and smiled. "I hear ya. Again, I am truly sorry for trespassing, er, Your Majesty. If you'll allow us, we will be on our way."

"Ah see no reason for tha'," Nolan said. They tensed again. "Wouldn't yeh like tae stay where yeh are? Rhys tells me yeh found a nice little farm house." Nolan nodded at Rhys.

"It was out near Balsam."

"Tha's a nice area," Nolan mused.

"It was nice, sir," Drake said sadly.

"Then why leave?"

Drake and Deandra exchanged confused glances.

"What he means is, stay and be one of us. Be a citizen of Blue Valley," Jane said. Nolan nodded.

Drake raised a skeptical brow. "Really?"

"O' course! There aren't many o' us left in this world. We have tae help each other. Protect each other. Tell me, what did yeh dae for a living before everything ended?"

"I was a preacher in Louisiana. We've been making our living the same way since then. We offer spiritual guidance in exchange for food and shelter."

"A spiritual man! In tha' case, ah must beg you tae stay here in town wi' us. We'll save the farm for yeh in Balsam, but ah'm hoping yeh might be willing tae take over the church here. It's a big, beautiful church, n' it's such a shame for it stand empty. Yer presence and yer guidance would be much appreciated."

Drake looked at Deandra. She shrugged. He looked back at Nolan. They could tell he was genuine and serious, but they still weren't sold. "What's the catch?"

Nolan stood. "There really isn't one. Yer expected tae grow yer oon food, hunt yer oon meat. If yer neighbors are in need, help them. If yer in need, they will help yeh. Dae yeh have weapons of yer oon?"

"We have a rifle and a couple of knives."

"We'll get yeh another firearm. There are only two solid rules in Blue Valley. First, dinnae take tha' which is not freely given. Ah cannot, ah will not, abide by theft. Yeh are tae settle any disputes amongst yerselves. Ah dinnae have time tae judge every little case, but big grievances, murder, theft n' the like, ye bring tae me."

"Yes, sir."

"The second rule, if yer summoned, yeh report here tae me, weapon in hand. While yeh live here, yeh have oor protection. Likewise, yer expected tae provide protection for those that live here. Make sense?"

"Perfect sense."

"Other than tha', take care o' yerselves, take care o' yer neighbors, don't be a dick. Well? What dae yeh say? Will yeh stay wi' us?"

Drake and Deandra smiled. "Of course we will."

Nolan stood and extended his hand. "Well, then welcome tae Blue Valley! Now, go forth n' be fruitful n' multiply n' all tha'."

Drake and Deandra shook his hand and thanked him profusely. One of Nolan's men led them from the room to take them to the armory.

The last trial of the day was Emory. Nolan motioned for Jane to join him. Jane stood beside Nolan's chair as the Guards pushed Emory to his knees before them. His hands were cuffed behind his back. His nose had stopped bleeding but it was still squashed and crooked. It and his eyes were dark blue and purple.

Nolan curled his nose. "Yeh've been charged wi' theft n' attempted rape. How dae yeh plead?"

"Don't matter," Emory said. "You gonna charge me anyway."

"Yer absolutely right. Under normal circumstances, yeh'd be punished as follows: for the charge o' attempted rape, the letter R will be forcibly tattooed on yer forehead, n' for the charge o' theft, yer dominant hand will be cut off. But—" He looked up at Jane. "Ah believe ah'll allow Jane tae decide yer punishment."

Jane looked down at Nolan in surprise. "No, Nolan. That's your job. Not mine."

"Why not? This man attacked yeh, or tried tae anyway. There's no telling how many times he succeeded before yeh came along. Come tae think o' it, we could call tha' other lad in here…"

"No, please," Emory pleaded. "Look, I'm sorry. Please don't call Leonard in here. I'm guilty, okay? I stole from a lot of people. I'll pay the money back. I'll do whatever I have to do, just please don't cut my hand off. Or tattoo my head."

Nolan looked up at Jane. "Well? Yeh should have a say in his punishment."

Jane contemplated Emory. "You deserve the punishment Nolan described." Emory cried out. Jane continued, "But I've always believed that you have to be the change you see in the world. Begetting violence with violence is not how you create a peaceful world. So as much as you deserve to lose your hand and have your face tattooed, I'm going to ask for leniency."

Emory crawled forward and fell at Jane's feet. "Thank you! Oh God, thank you."

Jane stepped back in disgust. "You have to repay all of the fees you stole. Instead of the letter R, a small X should be tattooed between your eyes. And instead of cutting off your hand, you should have the last two fingers of your right hand cut off. Maybe next time, you'll remember the mercy that was shown to you."

Nolan smiled at Jane and motioned for the Guards to take Emory away.

"Yeh were very lenient."

Jane shrugged. "I can't bring myself to be harsh, even against someone like him."

"Yeh haven't changed a bit."

"Yeah, well, neither have you."

"Ah'm very glad tae have yeh back, lass. Yeh helped us so much before yeh left. Yeh really must stay."

"We've got to get Duke to the doctor."

"Yes, yes, of course. But when he's healed, it'll be nice tae have yeh around."

"You mean it'll be nice to have your bookkeeper back."

"No, no. Well, yes, tha'," he laughed. Jane rolled her eyes. "Yer a good friend, Jane. Good people are hard tae come by these days."

"I know. I promise, we'll be back as soon as we can."

Chapter Six

"Hey. There you are. We've been looking for you." Duke came into the library.

Jane was sitting sideways in one of the reading chairs, her bare feet dangling over the arm. She looked up from a well-worn copy of *The Hobbit*. "Well, you found me."

"They fixed the road. We can leave in the morning."

Jane closed her book and stood. "Thank God. I'm gonna go start packing my stuff."

Duke brushed her off. "Do that in the morning. We're going down to the bar to have a drink before we go. You should join us."

"I dunno. I think I'd rather just stay here."

"Aw, c'mon, Jane. Don't be such a party pooper. When was the last time you actually let go and had fun?"

"I was having fun, with my book, til you came in here."

"I mean real fun. Like, wake up wearing somebody else's pants, can't remember what happened, kind of fun."

Jane raised an eyebrow and just looked at him.

"Exactly. Now c'mon. Let's go let go a little bit." Duke wrapped his good arm around her shoulders and steered her out the door. Jane sighed and let him.

The sun had disappeared behind the mountains. Twilight was rapidly fading into night as they climbed down the monumental stairs leading to the street. At the bottom of the stairs was a large round pool of murky water. Jane remembered when the water was crystal clear and the fountains in the middle danced and bubbled softly. On more than one occasion, she had sat on the bench by the retaining wall with a book she'd just checked out from the library, listening to the soft babbling of the fountain.

Old-fashioned gas lamps had been hung from the useless electric lamp posts, washing the sidewalk in patches of dim yellow light that shimmered and danced on the large store front windows. At the far end of the street, white balusters stood erect across the middle of the street. Jane had seen them a handful of times in the past. They were used to close the street to vehicle traffic for art festivals and fairs. A soft, smattering rain began to fall. It fell faster and harder with each passing second so by the time they made it to the tavern, they were soaked to the bone.

Duke pulled her under an awning. A low fence separated a little patio with tables and chairs from the sidewalk. Above the door was a faded purple sign that read Lulu's Café. Inside it was warm and dry. Jane had only ever eaten here once, but it was much like she remembered, the purple walls and nondescript tables and chairs, the bar against the back wall, the dining room on the other side, separated from the bar by a short wall.

A haze of cigarette smoke hung above the many heads of people sitting around the few tables in the small space. The bar was surrounded by a crowd of people talking and laughing. The oil lamps on every table bathed the room in a warm, comforting golden glow. The warm light, the happy, convivial people, the musky scent of smoke and bourbon, Jane felt like she'd just stepped into a hobbit hole. She felt more at home in this tavern than she had anywhere else in a long time.

Duke shook the rain from his hair and walked up to the bar. The men standing there greeted him loudly and handed him a brown bottle with no label. He gestured to Jane to join him. Jane took a sip from the bottle Duke handed her. It was a crisp apple cider. The spicy hints of cinnamon warmed her from the inside out.

Jane wandered into the dining room, looking for Willa. She was at a table in the back corner near the kitchen door. She was in the middle of a poker game with Rhys and Troy. They were laughing and chatting and seemed to have buried the hatchet. Each of them had a hand of cards and a pile of poker chips. Willa's pile was much smaller than the others. She looked up and caught Jane's eye. The corner of Willa's mouth twitched; her eye fluttered in an imperceptible wink. Jane shook her head. Willa nodded.

Jane raised her eyebrows. *You're gonna piss them off.*

Willa wrinkled her nose. *Nah, I got this.*

Jane rolled her eyes. *Don't say I didn't say I told you so.*

Jane wandered back toward the front window. She sipped her cider, watching the rain lash against the window in waves as the wind howled through the streets. Duke's voice filtered through the room.

"I'm telling you. She can drink you under the table and still wake up without a hangover."

"You're full of shit, man. Willa, maybe. But not Jane. There's no way."

"Wanna make a bet? That Panthers cap of yours looks like it would fit me just right."

"Alright. But when I win, you owe me a silver dollar."

"Deal. Jane. Hey, Jane! C'mere." Duke didn't wait for her to come. The crowd parted around him as he strode over to her.

"Show this guy how well you can hold your liquor."

Jane gave him a long-suffering look. "No, Duke. I'm not doing that."

He leaned in close. "I bet a silver dollar. I don't have a silver dollar. I can't lose this."

"See? I told you," the guy said.

"And who exactly are you?"

"Tyler." Tyler stuck his chin out and put his thumbs in the waist band of his nut-hugging Wranglers. A crowd of people had begun to ring around them, wondering what Jane would say.

"Well, Tyler." Jane started to tell him that she wouldn't do it, but his smug look rubbed her the wrong way. "Well, Tyler, get ready to give up that hat."

The crowd whooped, and Duke clapped her on the shoulder. Through the crowd, Jane caught Willa's eye.

She cast a glance at Tyler and shrugged. *Time to take him down a notch.*

Willa struggled to suppress a grin and nodded.

Jane followed Duke and Tyler back into the main room. The bartender set up a line of shot glasses on the bar. Jane pushed a stool aside and stood at the bar. Tyler, not to be outdone, copied her. The bartender poured each of them three shots of vodka. Tyler motioned for Jane to go first.

"Ladies first."

Jane shrugged, picked up the first glass, and knocked it back. One after another, Jane downed all three shots, slamming the glass down upside down after each one. She didn't flinch. Tyler looked at her, wide-eyed.

"Wasn't expecting that, were ya bud?" Duke laughed. "Go on. Your turn."

Tyler slammed down the first two. On the third one, he clenched his eyes and made an ugly face as he drank it. He gasped and grunted, but he managed to put them down and gestured for the next round. By that point, most everyone in the bar knew about the wager and were straining to get a good look. More wagers were made. Most of the money was on Jane. The bartender lined up six more shots. Jane downed the first one, when there was a yell and a crash from the next room.

Jane knew it had something to do with Willa's poker game. She abandoned her other two shots and pushed through the crowd to the other room. Duke was hot on her heels. Rhys stood between Willa and the other player, fending off his punches and keeping him away from Willa. Willa grasped wildly around Rhys trying to reach the guy, yelling at him.

Duke rushed forward and grabbed Willa. He wrapped both

arms around her waist and lifted her completely off the floor. Willa stopped flailing but continued to yell.

"You sorry sack of shit! How dare you accuse me!"

Rhys grappled with the other player, each struggling for an opening to swing. Jane reached up and grabbed the man's hair. He stumbled backward as he pulled back to swing at Rhys. Jane grabbed his arm and twisted it behind him. She kicked him in the back of his knee, forcing him to the ground.

"Ow! Goddammit!" he cried.

"Stop yelling," Jane said calmly.

"What are you doing to me? Let me go." He twisted and writhed, trying to escape her grasp, but Jane twisted his hair tighter around her fingers.

Jane twisted his arm a little more. "I said. Stop. Yelling."

He whimpered, but finally stopped resisting.

"Now. Tell me what happened." She continued to talk calmly to him but didn't release her grip.

"She cheated!"

"How do you know that?"

"I dunno. First, she was losing, then she just won everything. She hustled me."

"And, of course, there's no possible way she could've just been better than you."

"She was losing. She hustled me!"

"Don't tell me. Tell her."

"What?" The guy tried to turn around to look at Jane.

"You're gonna talk this out. Tell her. Say 'I am upset because I feel like you cheated.'"

The guy managed to twist around enough to look at Jane in bewilderment. "What the hell are you talking about?"

Jane forced him back around to face Willa. Duke had set her back on her feet. Willa crossed her arms. She was no stranger to Jane's "talk it out" approach. More than once, Jane had had to intervene between her and Duke.

The guy stewed silently, trying to understand what was going on. Finally, he said through gritted teeth, "I am upset because I feel like you cheated."

Jane looked at Willa like a teacher mediating an argument between fourth graders. "Willa?"

"Really? You're really gonna do this?"

Jane ignored her question. "Willa? How would you like to respond to Troy?"

Jane looked expectantly at Willa.

Willa rolled her eyes. "I respond by saying that I am sorry for making him feel like I cheated. I had several shitty hands in the beginning, but my luck turned. I understand it may have looked like I hustled him."

"Troy, do you accept Willa's apology?"

"Only if she gives me my money back."

"Hell no! I won that money fair and square. He's just a sore loser."

Jane gave her a long-suffering look. *Just do it, Willa.*

"Okay, fine." She sighed. "It's on the floor over there with all the rest of the game."

Jane relaxed her grip on Troy. "You heard her. Your money is over there. Go clean up the mess."

"Why do I have to do it?"

"Because you flipped the damn table. You made the mess. You clean it up. She gave you your money back. You clean up the mess. That's fair. Now go."

Troy glared at her but turned and started cleaning up the mess, muttering to himself the whole time. Jane went back to the bar. The entire crowd stared at her. She knocked back the last two shots, grabbed the hat off Tyler's head and shoved it into Duke's chest on her way out the door.

Jane noticed that Duke looked a little pale. He had aggravated his injury during the fight last night, and the less than clean atmosphere they had spent the last week living in didn't help. She handed him the water bottle she'd been drinking out of. It was full of blue liquid.

"What is it?" he asked warily. After Jane left the bar, he and Tyler had embarked on their own drinking contest. Duke was still a little drunk.

"Homemade Gatorade." He looked at her in confusion. "Powdered Kool-Aid with salt."

Duke took a swig from the bottle, then tipped it back and chugged it.

They were standing in front of the motel, packing up their last few belongings onto their horses. Nukem bounced between the three of them, pushing his nose into their palms, begging for ear scratches. They decided to leave the pack mule with Nolan. Jack had been a great help, but there was an unspoken, building sense of urgency. Jack would only slow them down. Willa was helping Duke mount his horse one handed when Nolan approached Jane.

"Before yeh leave, might ah ask a favor?" Nolan pulled a folded piece of paper from his pocket.

"Of course, Nolan. What's up?"

"Would yeh mind stopping by the Campus n' delivering this tae a man named Chuck?"

Jane took the note. "Of course. I'd be happy to."

Nolan smiled. "In this world, yeh have tae treat every goodbye as if it's yer last. I'm glad that wasn't the case this time, n' ah hope that it won't be in the future."

"I'm happy to see you too, Nolan."

"You're always welcome here All three of you." Rhys looked around at Willa and Duke.

"Thank you, Rhys. We'll be back as soon as we can." Willa said.

"You will, at any rate," Duke muttered. Willa hit him.

They mounted their horses.
"We'll see you around," Jane said.
"Take care o' yerselves," Nolan said.

Chapter Seven

Western Carolina University, once a thriving teaching college, stood between Sylva and Cashiers Village. As they came around the corner of the campus, Jane could clearly see that it was not abandoned. Far from it. The sports fields were blanketed in various crops, dotted with the brown sun hats of the people tending and harvesting them. Some of the people stood and waved. Jane smiled cautiously and waved back.

"Oh my God," Willa said softly. "Nolan wasn't kidding." She stared at the nearest field. It was full of hundreds of marijuana plants, waving at them in the breeze.

"Holy mother of ganja..." Duke said in awe.

At the entrance to the campus, they were stopped by two Guards with rifles.

"Leonard! What's up, buddy?" Duke cried.

Nuke trotted up to Leonard. Leonard bent down and scratched him behind the ears. Nuke wagged his bushy tail.

Leonard smiled widely and waved. He turned to his fellow Guard. "I know these guys. They're the ones that brought me to town. Hi, guys."

"What are you doing here, Leonard?" Jane asked.

"Nolan sent me here," he replied. "What are ya'll doing here?"

"Doing a favor for Nolan. We came to see Chuck."

"Oh, he's over in the dining hall helping set up a new still.

C'mon, I'll take you there."

Jane and Willa dismounted. "You okay, Duke?"

They turned to look at him. He hadn't moved to dismount and looked decidedly pale. "I think I'll just ride over there."

Jane gave Willa a concerned glance. *He's getting worse.*

Willa returned the look with an imperceptible shrug. *There's nothing we can do. We just need to hurry.*

"You look better," Willa said to Leonard as they walked. "Happier."

"I am. I can't thank you guys enough. You saved my life. If I'd stuck with Emory, I would've died."

"What makes you say that?"

Leonard studied his shoes. "I was in a bad place when I met Emory. I was on some hard drugs. He strung me along. 'Just help me rob these people, and I'll give you a hit,' he'd say. 'You gotta help me kill this guy. I'll get you more if you help me.' I was too deep to say no."

"Jesus, Leonard," Jane said.

"You looked pretty strung out when we met you," Willa said. "I could tell you were in bad shape."

Leonard continued to stare at his feet. "Nah, that was mostly withdrawal and cold shivers. Emory ran out of his stash a month ago." He looked up at Willa. "But I'm here now. I'm actually in a rehab group. That's why Nolan sent me here. They're helping me get clean."

"That's great. I'm proud of you," Willa said.

Leonard blushed and grinned.

"This place is incredible," Jane said.

"Yeah, it is. I'm not allowed to work with any of the product yet, since I'm still in rehab. That's why I'm on guard duty."

Willa raised a skeptical brow. "They put a recovering addict on guard duty?"

Leonard shifted the rifle slung over his shoulder. "It's not real. It's just a theater prop. They just gave it to me for show. Anyway," he said, changing the subject, "they make all kinds of stuff here."

Jane picked up on his lead. "Yeah, Nolan said they made liquor and beer."

"Oh, more than that. They use the science labs to make medicines too. We don't even have to grow food crops. People come from all over to trade for the stuff we make. They have a great reputation for quality products."

They crossed the now dry fountain and headed down the hill to the dining hall. There were people everywhere, crisscrossing the large courtyard. Six or seven men with toolboxes were headed in the same direction they were, towards the dining hall. An exhausted-looking group were headed up the hill towards the dormitories. Dozens of young people, not much older than teenagers, were laughing and horsing around as they headed toward the fields. A team of women nodded at them as they passed. They were laden with laundry baskets full of linens that smelled like rosemary and lavender.

"That is wild." Jane was astounded.

"It's an amazing place. We live in the dorms. Everybody has a job to do. We all receive and contribute fairly. If someone doesn't pull their weight, they're kicked out."

Willa seemed surprised. "People steal drugs and all they get is kicked out?"

"Well, no. They do leave with a, uh, reminder." Leonard giggled. "But Chuck doesn't believe in violence. He's one of those 'free love' kind of hippies."

"Do they have to give 'reminders' often?" Jane asked.

"I don't think so. They don't have that much trouble, from what I'm told. The last guy to try something was over a year ago. Donnie says they roughed him up a little but didn't really hurt him. They just kicked him out with nothing but the clothes on his back."

"Well, in this world, that's as good as a death sentence for some people," Jane said.

"You got a point, there," Leonard replied. As they approached the building, Duke opted to stay outside with the horses. Leonard eyed him with concern. They found Chuck on the first floor, overseeing the installation of a massive tank. Chuck was a quintessential hippie, with his long brown hair pulled back in a ponytail and a thick full beard, both streaked with gray. Even as the weather faded into fall, he wore khaki board shorts, a faded pink shirt, and sandals.

Leonard introduced them. Jane shook his hand and gave him the note. He opened it, his expression quizzical and disbelieving.

"He's batshit crazy if he thinks that's a fair trade," Chuck said, more to himself than anything.

"Yeah, well, this is Nolan we're talking about," Willa said.

"Did you read the note?" he asked.

"No, but I don't have to. We know Nolan well enough to know that he's batshit crazy."

Chuck laughed. "You're damn right he is. That's probably why he sent you with the note. Nobody to take my reply back to him so I can't argue." Chuck shook his head. "That old fart. Jeez." He turned to Leonard. "I'll be sending you back to him with my reply in a little bit."

Chuck walked with them back to their horses. Duke nodded to him, but didn't seem capable of much else.

"You okay, buddy?" Chuck asked.

"Not really," Duke said, "but thanks for asking."

"We're on our way to Cashiers Village to take him to the medical center," Willa explained.

Chuck approached Max and Duke. "Do you mind if I take a look?"

Duke winced as he carefully unbuttoned his shirt, pulled it back, and pushed aside the bandages. The three long gashes were bright red now and seeping pus. They were swelling and straining against the stitches.

"It's all we can do to keep it clean. We don't have any antibiotics," Jane said.

Chuck nodded. "I don't have much, but maybe I can get you something to help 'til you get up the mountain. It'll take you at least two days to get there from here on horseback. It's a pretty steep climb. Come with me." Chuck led them back across the courtyard to the student center.

Duke draped his good arm around Chuck's shoulders, but that was about all he could manage. Chuck grabbed his wrist and helped him hobble inside. He turned to a young woman with a smattering of freckles across her nose.

"Stephanie, I need you to bring me a bottle of whiskey, a mortar and pestle, a large stack of sterile bandages, enough for two days, a bottle of olive oil and…" He did a quick count in his head. "Five heads of garlic."

She returned his smile and went off to collect the odd assortment of items. Duke dropped into a chair and clenched his eyes shut. Nuke dutifully sat at his feet.

"I'll show you how to make a garlic dressing," he told them. He approached Duke and pointed at his shoulder. "May I?"

"Be my guest."

Chuck unwrapped Duke's shoulder. His long, dexterous fingers pulled the bandages away with barely a flinch from Duke. When Stephanie returned, he deftly peeled a couple of cloves of garlic, ground them in the pestle, and mixed it with the olive oil. The Campbells and Leonard watched in fascination. He spread the concoction on a gauze bandage, folded it over, and wrapped it around Duke's shoulder.

"The garlic and the olive oil are natural antibiotics. They won't cure you, I'm afraid, but it'll stave the infection off long enough for you to get to Cashiers Village." He handed Duke the bottle of whiskey. "Bottoms up."

Duke took a swig. "What's the whiskey do?"

"It keeps you drunk enough not to notice the pain."

Duke gave an approving nod. "Cheers." He downed another swig.

Chuck turned to Jane and Willa. "It's not much, I'm afraid, but I hope it will help."

"It's more than we expected," Jane said.

"And more than we deserve," Willa added. "Thanks, Chuck."

"Anytime," he said. "Any friend of Nolan's is a friend of mine." He checked his watch, "You still have plenty of daylight left to make a good head start. Like I said, it's a steep climb up that mountain. It'll take a couple of days. The garlic compress should be changed every four or five hours. For the size of his wound, crush two cloves and add enough oil to make a paste."

"Got it. Anything else?"

Chuck glanced at Duke, who had his head laid back on the couch, his eyes clenched shut and a sheen of sweat on his forehead. He turned back to the sisters and lowered his voice. "Keep him drunk and hurry. It won't be long until it turns septic. If it does, there's only a 50/50 chance he'll survive it."

Chuck helped Duke back outside to his horse. Duke lifted his foot to put it in the stirrup. He swayed on the spot, his weak grasp failed to hold onto the saddle. He missed and began to keel over backward. Chuck rushed forward and caught him. He held Duke upright. Duke grabbed the back of the saddle and steadied himself.

"You got this, man?"

"Yeah," Duke said. "Yeah, I'm good. Just...dizzy."

He managed to get his foot in the stirrup but stopped. He stood still, his head hung low, taking long deep breaths.

"C'mon, dude," Willa said. "We're wasting daylight."

"I...I, uh," he stuttered. "I can't." He spoke so softly, they almost didn't hear him.

"What?" Chuck asked.

He put his foot down and whispered to Chuck, "I don't have the strength to pull myself up." Jane and Willa didn't hear what he said, but they could hear the shame in his voice.

Chuck patted his good shoulder. "It's all good, man. Can you hold yourself up for a minute?"

Duke nodded. Chuck let him go and walked over to Jane and Willa.

A.J. Stewart

"Yeah, that's not happening. I've got an idea, though. Hold tight."

He took off at a run, yelling at someone to help him. He returned a few minutes later pushing an odd-looking wheelbarrow. It was longer and wider than a normal wheelbarrow; it was flat and had two wheels instead of one. The handles were longer and had heavy leather straps tied around the ends.

"This is one of our harvest carts," he explained. "One of our guys built several of them from scratch. I can have him make us another one. Ya'll need it more than we do."

He wheeled it around and behind Max. After a few minutes, the cart was hitched to Max's saddle. Stephanie came out with a worn comforter and laid it on the cart. Chuck helped Duke onto the cart. He laid back and groaned in relief.

"That's awesome, Chuck. Thank you," Jane said.

Jane checked on Duke one last time before they left. The fact that he didn't protest the cart and insist on riding worried her more than the fact that he needed it in the first place. He had one hand on his chest and his head turned to one side. His eyes were clenched shut in a painful grimace.

"Okay," Jane said. "Let's go."

Chapter Eight

Momma Dee stacked up the dishes and was heading toward the kitchen when she heard something outside. In the midst of the usual hubbub and general traffic, there was an unusual note of excitement. Something was coming, but it didn't have the same foreboding feel that accompanied the arrival of the Guards last year.

She set the dishes by the sink, wiped her hands on her jeans. and walked out onto the porch. Closing in on her sixtieth birthday, Momma Dee was a tall, strong woman. Thick-skinned and vulgar, everybody knew not to bullshit her. She twisted her long, thick hair into a clip on the back of her head.

The crowd in and around the intersection didn't look any different, but there was still that feeling in the air that something was coming. She looked back up the road toward the compound. She couldn't see it from where she was, but just the knowledge that it was there was enough to set her mood off.

It had once been the Ingles shopping center. Now, it housed the National Guard. They had erected a chain link fence topped with curls of razor wire all the way around it and the cleared lot across the street. The wide gates that spanned the road were perpetually manned by armed Guards. The large sloping parking lot housed their unnecessarily large fleet of trucks and Jeeps. Nobody was sure what they had in there, and no one was dumb enough to go in and find out.

Momma Dee shrugged and walked back into the little restaurant market she managed. Whatever it was, it would find her soon enough. Everybody that came through Cashiers Village always found their way to Momma Dee's. Whether it was to buy, sell, trade, or just see what Momma Dee had cooked up that day, the Market was the centerpiece of the Village. And as its matron, Momma Dee heard everything about everybody.

A young boy came into the kitchen. He perched his lanky frame on a stool at the large steel table and propped his elbows on the table.

"What's going on at the crossroad, Oscar?" she asked.

"Somebody was seen coming up the road from Sylva," he said, eyeing the basket of apples in front of him.

Momma Dee scowled. "Who?"

He picked an apple and bit into it. "I dunno," he said around a mouthful of fruit. "Everybody's making a big deal about it though. They keep talking about how they're 'unharmed.'"

"That is strange," she mused. "Here, go get some water. I need to get these dishes cleaned before the supper run." She handed him a bucket and shooed him out the back door.

The last time anyone came down that road was over a year ago. The man was beaten so badly he didn't survive more than three days. That was the whole point of the agreement. The Valley Boys protected the northern border and the Guard left them alone. Granted, they took their job a little too seriously, rarely letting anyone through at all, but all the same, it was a solid agreement that everyone abided by. So all that was left was that all pressing question: who in God's name had enough influence to pass through Valley Boy territory without a scratch?

Oscar came back in with the bucket, water sloshing onto the floor. He set it on the floor by the sink.

"The Guards seemed really pissed about it," he continued.

"Watch your mouth."

"Sorry. A whole bunch of them loaded up in a truck and rode out there to meet them. Probably gonna arrest 'em or something."

Momma Dee dumped the water into the sink and added soap. "I wouldn't doubt it. Those assholes are always making a big deal out of things. How many were there?"

"Travelers or Guards?"

"Both."

"I think somebody said there was three people coming. I saw about eight Guards get in the truck."

Momma Dee pursed her lips. She knew those Guards were trouble from the first day they showed up. Most of them meant well; they came through the market nearly every day. The majority of them were nice enough, just doing what they're told. Some of them, though...some of them were just a little too eager with punishments. They almost seemed to relish in it.

Momma Dee shook her head. She grabbed a plate and plunged it into the water. "You ought to head home, Oscar. You need to get your school work done."

"Okay, Momma Dee. You need me to do anything else before I go?"

"That's okay, hun. I got it. You go get your homework done."

"Okay. I'll be back tomorrow."

"Thanks, Oscar. And hey, tell your momma I got those new wash basins. I'll bring them over to her sometime today."

"OK. I will." Oscar pushed the stool back under the counter and went out the back door.

Just as Chuck predicted, it took them two days to climb the mountain to the Village. Jane led Max by a lead rope. Over the last twenty-four hours, Duke's condition nosedived. He had spiked a fever overnight. His skin was burning hot, but he shivered in a cold sweat. It was warm during the day but temperatures were starting to plummet at night. Jane and Willa sacrificed their blankets for him, but they didn't seem to help.

They came around the lake on the third day. The heavy fog that settled on the water was beginning to dissipate in the late morning sun. Two trucks came barreling down the road towards them. National Guard soldiers stood in the beds of the trucks, guns raised. They came to a stop sideways in the road, blocking the way. A few young boys fishing from a dock stopped to watch as the guards jumped down from the bed of the truck, lined up in the road and raised their guns.

"Stop right there!" one yelled.

They stopped. Jane bit down on the inside of her lip, chewing on it until the skin was ragged and tender. Willa's eyes flitted between Jane and the Guards, unsure of what to do. Duke's eyes fluttered half open at the sudden stop. He muttered something unintelligible about a cat. Nuke growled.

Jane looked to Willa. *What do we do?*

Willa looked wide-eyed back at Jane. She shrugged and pointed at her. *Are you kidding me? This is your turf. You do something.*

The grasshoppers were back. She took a deep, shaky breath to steady herself and turned back to the line of Guards. She put her trembling hands in the air as a signal of peace.

"My name is Jane Campbell." She tried to keep her voice calm, but a shiver of fear shuddered through her body, making it shake. "These are my siblings. We are citizens of Cashiers Village."

"State your business," the Guard demanded.

"We have been traveling for three years, but we have decided to return home. My brother is in desperate need of medical attention," she said. "You can verify our identities with other locals in town when we get there, but I really do need to get Duke to a doctor."

The leader of the Guards pointed his rifle at her knees rather than her chest and stepped forward. "Dismount your horses. You will get in the truck, and we will take you to the processing center. Your horses will be taken and held in the public stable. Your belongings will be searched. Anything that is deemed necessary for the community will be confiscated. Everything else will be returned to you after processing."

Jane was taken aback, but Willa was livid. "What the hell is all this? You can't just take our horses and our stuff!"

"We can, and we will, ma'am," the Guard replied. "If you want access to the Village that is. It's safety protocol."

Willa opened her mouth, but Jane shushed her. "Just go along with it. This is what Nolan warned us about, remember?"

Willa fell into a seething silence. She cooperated but not without furious, grudging glances at the Guards. They handed their reins over to one of the Guards and climbed into the bed of the truck. Duke sat with his back against the cab. His breathing was shallow and his face was paler than ever. Jane pulled back the bandage on his shoulder. His swollen skin stretched between her crude stitches. Jane's own shoulder throbbed in sympathetic pain. Blood and pus seeped. The stench of infection and garlic was overwhelming.

"It's getting worse," Willa said unhelpfully. She braced herself as they rounded a corner.

"We're almost in town," Jane whispered to Duke. "Just hang in there."

The truck pulled into the parking lot between Buck's Coffee Café and the visitor's center. The Guards grabbed Jane and Willa by the arm and yanked them out of the bed. Jane stumbled and scraped her knees on the pavement. The Guard jerked her back up on her feet. Willa's Guard shoved her inside the visitor's center. A curious crowd began to gather.

"Watch it, asshole," Willa snapped. She elbowed the Guard herding her inside.

It took two men to carry Duke inside. Nuke tried to follow them, but one of the Guards kicked him aside. Nuke snarled, but the Guard ignored him. There was another Guard waiting inside. His blond hair was buzzed into a military flat top. The insignia on his chest labeled him as a Sergeant. His name tag said Smith.

"Sit and wait" was the order. "You will all have a medical evaluation after processing."

"What about my brother? I told you he needs a doctor!" Jane was becoming more and more agitated.

"And I told you he will see one after he is processed."

"What is this processing bullshit?" Willa demanded.

"We have to determine that you are not a threat to the community. Especially since you came straight down from an area inhabited by very hostile people. You will be subjected to a series of medical and psychological exams while members of the community will be interviewed to corroborate your story."

"Great, can Duke have his medical exam first?"

"No, the medical exams come last. If we determine you are a threat, we will send you out of the community and there will be no need to waste time on a medical exam if that is the case."

"THIS IS HORSESHIT! HE NEEDS A DAMN DOCTOR!" Willa was on her feet, screaming.

The sergeant took a rifle from a Guard nearby and drove the butt of it into her stomach. It knocked the wind out of her, and he pushed her back into her seat.

"You see, it is precisely this type of behavior that gets one labeled as a threat," he said, handing the gun back.

Jane scowled at Sergeant Smith as he strode away. "Please, Willa. Just keep it under control until this is over. It's the only way to get Duke to a doctor."

"What the hell happened to this place? It wasn't like this when we left."

"I know, I know. But in order to find out, we have to be allowed back into the Village. For that, we have to go through this processing thing. And to do *that,* you have to keep your temper under control. Comprendé?" Jane's tone became more and more stern with each word. Willa took notice and backed down.

She frowned at Jane. "Yeah, yeah, yeah. I comprendé."

The processing, took hours. Several other people came through to be processed but they were in and out in half an hour. For whatever reason, they were dragging it out for the Campbells.

Jane sat across the table from yet another Guard, this one with thin rimmed glasses and a clipboard.

"State your name."

"Jane Elizabeth Campbell."

"That is not the name we have on file."

"If you have my name on file, why did you ask?"

The Guard glared at her. "Just answer the question."

"You didn't ask one." Jane wiped her sweaty palms on her jeans. She could feel her pulse thudding in her throat. What was wrong with her? She usually wasn't this snide.

"My legal name, that you have on file, is Kraus."

"Why didn't you say that to begin with?"

"Habit. I've been using my maiden name for several years."

"Why?"

"It was easier. Since I've been traveling with my family, I thought it would be easier to use the family name rather than have to explain it. I thought wrong, apparently. Willa did the same thing."

"It says here you were a legal resident of Cashiers Village."

"Yes, I have a home I shared with my husband on the other side of the lake."

"And where is your husband?"

"Dead," she whispered. Losing him had been hard, so she avoided talking about it whenever she could.

He had the good grace to look a little ashamed. "Oh, I'm sorry. We will send a Guard to accompany you to your home when you are ready to return there. Since it's been abandoned for several years, we would like to conduct a safety inspection to ensure that it is still habitable. If you have anything there that can be used to help the community as a whole, it will be confiscated. I know it's been a while since you've been there, but do you recall if there is anything there that can be used for the community? Medication? Weapons?"

Jane chewed on her bottom lip and hid her trembling hands beneath the table. "No. We took everything with us when we left." She avoided looking him in the eye, but he didn't seem to notice.

"The Guard tells me that your brother and sister had several firearms in their possession, but not you. You only carried a bow and a quiver of arrows. Why is that?"

"They're better shots than I am."

"But surely a gun is a much better weapon than a bow."

Jane shifted uncomfortably in her chair. There was a perfectly good reason why she didn't carry a gun, but she wasn't about to share her life story with this asshole.

"I just don't like guns," she said.

"Is there anything else we should know about? If we find that you are withholding information, you will be persecuted." His tone wasn't stern but rather clinical and uncaring.

Jane swallowed the lump in her throat. "No. Nothing." Finally, after four hours of questioning, poking, and prodding, they were deemed to be of no threat. Indeed, they were upstanding citizens of Cashiers Village and very much missed by many. The government had no reason to continue holding them so they were released, and their belongings returned to them. They did not, however, have time to go through and see what they kept from their stuff.

As soon as they stepped out of the processing center, they were swept up in a cheering mob of people. At least forty people were there; some of them were just curious onlookers, but many of them familiar faces who were ecstatic to see them, especially Jane, alive. Jane and Willa tried to make themselves heard over the cacophony of cheers and well wishes but to no avail. Willa gave up and screamed until the crowd fell into silence.

"Does anyone have a car or something that can take my brother to the doctor before he dies!"

"Over here," a lone voice called from the back of the crowd.

As if commanded by God, the crowd parted to reveal a small Hispanic woman standing next to a rusted-out Ford pickup.

"Thank you."

Willa helped Jane half lead, half carry Duke to the truck. Jane couldn't help but notice that the Guards that had helped carry him before were nowhere to be found. Dukes eyes rolled around in his head, and his eyelids fluttered. He rambled about getting new shoes for his cat.

He was falling in and out of consciousness. Since Duke had essentially become dead weight, the easiest thing to do was put him in the bed of the truck. Given that he was roughly the size of Andre the Giant, it was no easy task. With the help of a couple bystanders, they managed to get him in the truck. Willa hopped in the back with Duke while Jane climbed into the cab with their savior. Nuke leaped into the bed. He laid his head on Duke's lap and whimpered.

Chapter Nine

Before the Fall, it was the only place for medical care in Cashiers Village. Afterward, it continued to be so. Being a mile or so outside of town, it was close enough to be convenient, but far enough to be a safe place to quarantine the sick.

As they drove through the main intersection in town, Jane noticed for the first time how different things were since the last time she was here. Like the bodies, for instance. Jane couldn't stop staring at them as they passed. There were eight of them, hanging from the arms of the street lights going West and South. Mostly men, a couple women, and one boy who couldn't have been more than fourteen. She could only tell his age because he was the freshest. His blue, sunburned skin was not yet decayed and eviscerated like those hanging around him. The crows had yet to pluck out his eyes.

"You are a lifesaver, Maria." Jane sighed as she sank back into the seat. She could feel the springs through the worn-out padding of the seat. Maria drove out of town, past the country clubs, to the medical center. Rows and rows of graves had been dug on the golf green by the road. Jane could see people far back on the green digging more.

"Hey, it's no problem. I was just relieved to finally see you again. We all thought you were dead," Maria said. "Where the hell have you been, anyway?"

"It's a long story. The simple answer is we've been traveling. What the hell happened here?"

Jane looked over at Maria. Her long black hair was in a braid, pulled forward over her shoulder. She was a tiny woman. Her seat was pulled close to the steering wheel so she could reach the pedals.

"It's a long story. The simple answer is we were offered help and now we regret it." Maria sounded pissed.

They pulled into the parking lot at the medical center. Maria honked the horn and several people in lab coats came running out. Without explanation, they lifted Duke onto a gurney and wheeled him inside. Jane told Nuke to stay in the truck. He whined and paced in circles but stayed in the bed. A red-haired nurse with a purple stethoscope told Jane and Willa to wait in the lobby. The three women sank into the overstuffed chairs of the waiting room. Jane put her head in her hands.

"Did you see the fuc—"

"Yes, I saw the bodies," Jane interrupted Willa.

"What the hell, Jane? And who's our knight in shining armor?"

Jane looked up at Maria, then to Willa.

"This is Maria. We worked together Before. She's a damned good cook and an even better friend."

Willa extended her hand. "That's all I need to know. Thank you, Maria."

"You're most welcome. I just hope he's going to be okay."

"You and me, both," Jane whispered. She kept thinking about the stitches she gave him back in the woods. Had her shoddy medical care contributed to his infection?

Jane looked to Maria again. "What is going on here, seriously?"

Maria's eyes widened. She shook her head and glanced toward the darkened check in window.

"Not now," she whispered. "I'll tell you but not here. Wait til we get home."

Jane and Willa looked at Maria with deepening confusion. Not a moment later, the red-haired nurse came into the waiting room. Willa and Jane jumped to their feet. The nurse put up her hands.

"Before you ask, he's stable. But only just. Who is he? And who are you?"

Jane introduced herself and her sister. She explained Duke's injury and her makeshift sutures.

The nurse nodded. "That explains a lot. Well, the truth is, it's become septic. The amount of antibiotics he would need would wipe out most of our stocks. In cases like his, protocol is to make him as comfortable as possible but no more. Medication and antibiotics are reserved for more viable patients."

Willa exploded. "Are you kidding me? So you're just going to let him die?"

The nurse winced at Willa's shrill admonition. She did her best to placate her. "It is not unheard of for patients like him to fight off the infection and recover on their own. If his immune system is strong enough, he might pull through. But it is not sustainable to give our limited antibiotics to patients who may not make it. I am sorry. As soon as you have lodging, he will be released into your care. I can give you bandages, dressings, and a few painkillers but outside of that I am afraid we cannot help you."

Willa stared at the nurse in disbelief for a long moment, then spit in her face. Jane grabbed Willa and pushed her backward into a chair.

"Goddammit, Willa. Can you not keep your temper in check for one goddam minute?"

"But that redheaded bitch—" Willa flung her arms wide, pointing at the door the nurse had disappeared through.

Jane put her head close to her sisters and spoke in a harsh whisper. "That redheaded bitch is just doing her damn job. I can guarantee that she didn't make the call. Don't take it out on her. We're already targets in this town. You saw the bodies. Somebody's in control who does not give damn about you, me, or Duke. Until we figure out who it is and what they're doing, Keep. Your. Mouth. Shut."

Willa lapsed into a resigned but furious silence.

When Jane turned around, the nurse was gone.

"I told her ya'll would be staying with me. She went to go get your brother," Maria said. "I'm so sorry."

Maria put a comforting hand on Jane's arm. Jane hugged her, but her smile was tired and weak.

"Thank you again. At the very least, we'll have a place to stay while we figure things out. Where do you live?"

"At the Laurelwood Inn. I run the inn. I have a cabin in the back you guys can have."

"We've been sharing a tent for the last three weeks. At this point, we would've taken a bed in the hallway."

The red-haired nurse and two orderlies wheeled Duke into the lobby in a wheelchair. The orderlies helped put Duke back in the truck. He seemed fractionally more aware, doing his best to be a cooperative patient, but he was still delirious. He seemed to have forgotten about the cat shoes. The red-haired nurse, keeping her distance from Willa, approached Jane with a plastic bag.

"I really am sorry about your brother," she said. There was a pleading edge to her voice, as if she was worried. She glanced over at Duke with regret and Willa with trepidation. Turning back to Jane, she handed her the bag.

"That's all I could manage without anyone noticing," she whispered. "Don't open it here."

"What's your name?"

"Charlotte. But everyone calls me Charlie."

Jane gave her a reassuring smile. "Thank you, Charlie."

"I cleaned his wound as well as I could. It's as clean as it's gonna get. Your sutures were pretty good, by the way, given the circumstances. The infection would've been so much worse without them."

Willa called out to Jane, waving at her to hurry up.

"Good luck, Jane."

"Thank you again." Jane turned to leave.

"Jane?" Charlie called. Jane turned. "Let me know if he makes it."

Jane nodded and hurried to the truck. Once in the truck, Jane looked in the bag. There were rolls and rolls of bandages and a huge wad of dressing pads. She started to put the bag in the floor when she heard something rattle. Reaching in, she realized that one of the rolls wasn't as soft as the others. She unrolled it. Hidden inside was half of a bottle of antibiotics. Jane let out a relieved sigh. Taking Willa's abuse with grace, smuggling out drugs that might just save Duke's life. Charlie was an ally.

Chapter Ten

When they got back to the inn, Maria led them to a quaint little cabin at the back of the property. A beautiful staircase led to a loft with two beds. A couch with leaf patterns faced a propane fireplace in the small living room. Across from the little kitchenette, a bedroom and the only bathroom were tucked under the stairs. Everything was decorated with rustic touches, from the wood paneled walls to the laurel wood branches that made up the balusters on the stair railing.

They settled Duke on the bed in the bedroom under the stairs. He winced, his breathing shallow. Nuke turned in a few circles, laid at Duke's feet, and refused to leave his side. Willa sank into the couch and laid her head back. Maria bustled around the kitchen making coffee. Jane tried to help, but Maria shooed her away. Jane sat on a barstool at the counter. She put her elbows on the counter and held her head in her hands. On the counter was a laminated piece of green paper. Jane picked it up.

Welcome to the Laurelwood Mountain Inn

We're happy that you've chosen to stay with us. Here are a few things that we would like for you to know to make your stay more enjoyable.

It listed phone numbers, wi-fi passwords, TV guide channels, where to find towels, and sightseeing tips. It was jarring to see something so normal and yet so unfamiliar.

Maria brought back steaming cups for Jane and Willa.

"Is it safe to talk here?" Jane asked.

"Sí. There is no one listening here."

"What happened, Maria? Who are these people?"

Maria sighed. She was quiet for a long moment, trying to think of how to start. "They came about a year and a half ago. You remember the militia community from Clemson?"

Jane nodded.

"Well, they came and met with the council. They wanted to expand their army. Help protect surrounding areas. They came to Cashiers Village because it's one of the few safe places to cross the mountains. They said they wanted to help keep it that way."

"That sounds pretty good, actually," Willa said.

"Sí. We thought so too. We held a town meeting. Everyone agreed to additional security, but no more. We wanted to keep running the Village as we always had."

"That sounds good too, but it doesn't explain the shit show out there."

Maria nodded. "They accepted our terms and sent troops to provide security. But they kept sending more and more troops, more than we needed. More than we could support. The Guards began policing the villagers, punishing them. That wasn't part of the agreement. The council appealed to the militia leaders. They begged them to back off. That's when things went south. They essentially told us that the original agreement was out the window, that they were assuming control of the Village. We were to listen and obey the new leadership or suffer the consequences.

"But what about you? I left and went to Mexico, and when I came back you and Levi were gone. They told me ya'll had disappeared."

Jane nodded. This was exactly why she had avoided coming back to the Village. She had lost everything, including her husband, and had no desire to relive it. But Maria was her friend and Jane owed her an explanation.

"Right after you left, and I'm just talking days after, Willa came up here to get me. Our mother and Willa's little girl were sick. Willa didn't think they'd make it so she came to get me so I could see them one last time. I told Levi I would only be gone a few days and I left." Jane had to stop and steady her voice, as it had begun to shake. "But by the time we got back home, Emma had died and our mother had disappeared without a trace."

"Díos mío..."

But Jane wasn't done. "I came back to the Village to tell Levi we were leaving. There was a possibility that Momma was still alive and we had to find her. She'd been kidnapped."

"Oh Jane, lo siento mucho. Did you find her?"

Jane shook her head. "All of our leads told us there was a gang of people kidnapping people and selling them into slavery. We followed the trail all the way to Louisiana, but the trail went cold. Best we could figure, she was taken up the Mississippi River, probably taken out West."

"What about Levi?"

"He, uh," Jane faltered, "got sick on the way home. An infection just like...just like Duke. He didn't make it." She stared at her shoes. "By that point, we had been gone for months. There wasn't anything left for us back home so we just traveled. We went where we wanted, when we wanted. We rode all the way up and down the Eastern Seaboard. What about you? Did you find your family in Mexico?"

"Sí, I found them eventually. I never thought I'd say this, but I actually had to sneak across the border *into* Mexico. They've got the border locked down."

"If you made it out, why did you come back?" Willa asked.

"This is my home. Besides, I left my son, Oscar, here with a friend of mine. It was too dangerous to take him with me. I couldn't just leave him here."

"The Canadian border is shut down too. We heard a rumor that Canada was threatened by Russia not to help us," Willa said.

"Not just Canada and not just by Russia. North Korea, Russia, Iran, Pakistan, anyone that the United States screwed with. Under threat of receiving the same fate, all of our allies are forbidden from providing aid of any kind."

"Jeez. I didn't realize it was that bad."

"From what I understand, part of Brazil has already been bombed for sending a single supply ship."

"You're kidding."

Maria shook her head. "We're on our own with this. At this point, I'm not even worried about that. It's the wolf in our backyard that we need to do something about."

Chapter Eleven

Three days passed. Duke slid back into his delirium the day after they talked with Maria. Willa and Jane had been taking turns caring for Duke, cleaning his wounds, giving him his medicine, and trying to coax him into eating, even if it was just broth. Willa felt too cooped up in the little cabin. She needed air.

It had been a while since she's been in the Village, not that she had spent much time there in the first place. This had been Jane's home. She'd moved up here with her husband. Willa and Duke had lived in South Carolina, where they grew up. Well, Willa did. Duke had been living the glorious life of a football god at Appalachian State.

She crossed the street, through the parking lot of the old Exxon gas station. Inside she could see several Guards sitting at desks, like a central office. The park was on the other side of the road. She began to cross. A thunder of hooves on pavement came from her right, and she looked up. A solid white horse galloped past her toward and through the intersection. Several men on horseback chased after it. Willa watched until they were gone then continued across the street.

She wandered through the park, not really knowing where she was going. There were several children playing on the large playground. It occurred to her that even if their world hadn't ended, these children would still be playing on that playground. In that place, in that small moment, it was as if nothing had ever happened. She could almost see her baby girl playing with them.

Emma didn't deserve what happened to her. It was all Derek's fault. Willa remembered how all of them were starving. They hadn't eaten in days. They were all weak, but Emma didn't stand a chance. She was so sick. She needed a doctor. But Derek refused to leave. He was afraid if they left, someone would mug them. Attack them. Kill them. If they left they would die for sure. If they stayed at least they had a chance. He'd convinced himself that Emma would recover.

But she didn't. She just got worse and worse. Willa couldn't do anything. Derek had barricaded them in the basement. All she could do was watch her ex-husband lose his mind while Emma slowly faded away. Willa gave up trying to convince him. After a bloody fight with Derek that left him with a cracked skull, Willa bundled Emma up and broke out of the basement. But it was too late. She didn't stand a chance against whatever it was she had. Willa remembered holding her, her frail little body was like a trembling bundle of twigs as her last breath...

She turned and walked on before that thought could complete itself. Her chest ached every time she thought about it. The last thing she needed right now was to relive that loss.

The small field next to the park had been transformed into a garden, as had most available space around the Village. Having yards to play and picnic in was a luxury they could no longer afford. Every available space was needed to grow enough food to feed the ever-growing town.

She followed the overgrown gravel path around a covered picnic area and more gardens, lost in her thoughts. As she came around the corner, she was shaken from her thoughts by an unusual sight. A large, sprawling, *mowed* lawn. There were no gardens or overgrown grass. Just a pristine lawn next to a gravel parking lot. The lawn was crowned by a U-shaped open-air stage. There was a small office on one side and a storage building on the other.

Willa remembered Jane telling her about this place, but this was the first time she'd ever seen it. The stage had hosted free Friday night concerts. The lawn would've been covered with picnic blankets and folding chairs, families gathered for a summer evening filled with food and music. But considering the current state of things, it was eerie.

Willa continued on, past the post office and the Rec department. On the hill was another, smaller playground and a baseball field, both void of activity. Further down, another cluster of buildings. A thrift shop. A food pantry. The public swimming pool, full of murky, disgusting water. A long red building boasting a "Community Center" sign stood behind the Fire Department. She could hear voices coming from the front of the fire station.

There were two men standing in front of the Fire Station pouring over a large map spread across a table. As she approached she caught pieces of the conversation.

"I told you, there's nothing in there. We've been through that area a dozen times."

"Then what do you suggest, oh wise one?" The man was of average height, with a dark goatee and mustache flecked with gray.

"Shit, I dunno." The other man was much taller and darker. Puerto Rican, if she had to guess. He stood and stretched, putting his hands on top of his head. "But we've got to find medical supplies somewhere. They're starting to cut up t-shirts for bandages."

"Have you looked at the homes of the doctors and nurses?" Willa asked.

They both turned to look at her. They seemed eager for any lead they could get. They didn't seem at all upset that their conversation had been interrupted.

"What are you talking about?" the tall man asked. The Puerto Rican was just as tall as Duke, but leaner and longer legged, his hands wide enough to palm a beach ball. His dark hair had been twisted into long, thin dreadlocks.

"Well, I remember when my mom worked in a hospital. She was always bringing home supplies. Not major stuff. Little stuff like bandages, suture kits, saline solution. So after the Fall, when me and my brother and sister needed to find stuff to trade, we would go find the homes of doctors and nurses to see what kind of supplies they had stashed."

They stared at her in disbelief.

"That's brilliant."

Willa smiled. "All doctors' offices and hospitals have a staff directory. It's just a matter of taking the time to break into the records office and look up the information."

"What's your name?"

"Willa."

The tall guy extended his hand. "I'm Carlos. This is Darin. We're part of the Searchers. We go out and look for things we need."

Willa shook his hand. A woman stepped out of the community center. Through the open door, Willa could hear screams and yelling coming from inside. She panicked and ran toward the woman.

"Hey wait!" Carlos called.

"Someone is in trouble! Did you not hear the screaming?" Willa didn't stop. She ran past the woman, not noticing how calm she was.

The screams grew louder as she stepped inside. Yelling and running footsteps thundered overhead. Willa's heartbeat thundered in her ears. The guys from the Fire Station caught up with her just as she ran up the stairs.

"Wait. It's not what you—"

Willa stopped short in the doorway. Carlos and the woman from outside caught up to her. Willa found herself facing a basketball court. The yelling and running weren't people in trouble. It was a basketball game. A flock of teenagers chased each other up and down the court. On the sidelines, several small children played at the feet of just as many elderly people watching the game. A couple of middle aged women stood at the back, keeping an eye on everything.

"What is this?"

"We call it the Home," the woman explained. "A lot of people have died since the End. These kids were orphaned over the years.

We take care of them here." She nodded toward the elderly people. "They managed to survive, but they didn't trust themselves to live alone anymore. They help us with the kids when they can."

Willa turned to the woman. Her long auburn hair was braided down her back. Her nose was pierced, and she had several earrings along the edges of her ears. "Why didn't anyone in town take these kids in? Surely there's someone out there who would be willing to take one or two into their home?"

"Yeah, but many people don't receive rations from the National Guard. They only have enough to feed themselves. The Guard gives us weekly rations for each child. Here they have a reliable source of food. I'm Laura, by the way."

"Willa."

"Oh, you're one of the ones that came up from Sylva. Or Blue Valley, as they call it now. How did you manage that?"

"We've got friends in high places, I guess. So you're in charge here?"

"I guess you could say that. I'm supposed to be helping my mom run the market in town, but we get kids in here more and more lately. Somebody's gotta keep this place running."

"This is incredible." Willa thought of Emma again. "I'll help you in any way I can. Just say the word."

Chapter Twelve

"You look like hell."

Jane jerked up. Willa stood over her. She had been sitting on the floor in front of the coffee table reading a book. She must have fallen asleep.

"Shit. I'm sorry." She scrambled to stand up but her legs had fallen asleep from being crossed for so long. She fell back to the floor, flexing her ankles and knees. "What time is it?"

"Noon. How long have you been sitting there?"

"Well, I sat down last night around 9:30 with a candle to read."

The candle was out and nothing more than a nub in its stand.

"Dude, you need a break. You've been in this house for two days. Duke's not going anywhere. Why don't you go into town? There's a bunch of people asking about you."

"Who?"

"Well, for one, the lady at the Farmer's Market. And a lady at the Community Center. And some of the guys at the Fire Station."

This was precisely the reason Jane had stayed in the cabin. She had been avoiding facing her friends and neighbors. She was afraid of what they would say. Would they be mad that she had left? What rumors had been passed around? The authorities seemed more interested in, and more threatened by, her and her siblings than they should have been. More than anything, she was afraid of being swarmed. So many people with so many questions. She was afraid of the panic attack it would trigger. But she knew she would have to face them sooner or later. Might as well get it over with.

"Don't worry about it. It's not like you have to stay out there," Willa reminded her. She knew what Jane was thinking. "You don't have to explain yourself to anybody, either. If you need to leave, leave."

Jane relaxed a little. When her anxiety overwhelmed her, it always helped her to know she had a way out. An escape route.

"Okay. I'll go. But if you need me—"

"I'll be fine. Go." Willa pulled Jane to her feet.

"The antibiotics are hidden in my shoes, under my bag in my room. There are some clean bandages in the cabinet in the bathroom."

"I got it. Go see your friends."

"I won't be gone long. I'll be right back."

"GO!" Willa pushed her out the door.

"Okay. Okay." She laced up her boots and walked down to the street.

The Farmer's Market was across the intersection. Out of habit, she looked both ways before crossing the street. Feeling a little foolish, she jogged across the cracked asphalt.

Once upon a time, the Farmer's Market had been the best place in town for fresh local meat, vegetables and homemade everything. Jane's favorite was always the breads that were handmade every day and the barbeque they served from the window on the far side of the porch.

The open front of the Market revealed that the stands and aisles of vegetables had been replaced with two long tables which were beginning to fill with people as they sat down to lunch. The shelves that lined the walls were still filled with a variety of canned food, but the familiar Farmer's Market labels had been replaced with plain, handwritten stickers.

As Jane mounted the short set of steps, a portly man happened to turn and look in her direction. He did a double take.

"Hi, James." Jane took a deep breath. *Here goes nothing,* she thought.

"Jane?" His eyes widened. "Jane Kraus?"

Several more heads turned. Some of them turned back to their meals but others stared. There were only a couple of faces in the crowd that Jane recognized. The majority were strangers. Cashiers Village had always been a close-knit town. Everybody knew everybody, or at least recognized them. To be surrounded by people she had never seen was unsettling. Many of them stood and approached her.

"Oh my God! I heard you were back, but I didn't believe them," a sandy-haired man said. He wrapped his arms around her.

"Hi, Dave. Yeah, I'm back." She was reluctant to hug him, but she put on her best smile and ignored her fluttering heart.

"Where's Levi?" A bony woman wrapped her arms around Jane's shoulders in a delicate hug. Loretta always was a fragile woman.

"He, uh—"

"Jane? Is that you?" a loud, familiar voice rang out from the back of the crowd.

"Momma Dee," Jane sighed. The sea of people parted to reveal a tall woman in her late fifties with a lined face. Her long brown hair was pulled up in a clip. Jane could see how much Dee had aged since she had been gone. Her hair was liberally streaked with gray, and deep wrinkles creased in the corners of her eyes when she smiled. It was clear that Jane had no intention of answering the crowd's questions so they slowly made their way back to their tables, content with the knowledge that the prodigal daughter had returned, alive and well.

Jane ran forward and wrapped her arms around Dee's waist. Dee wrapped Jane in a strong hug. While she could be obdurate and forcefully opinionated, Momma Dee always had a warm, motherly nature that made everyone around her feel safe and loved.

Momma Dee pulled back and held Jane at arm's length and smiled at her. "Girl, I thought I'd never see you again."

"I'm sorry, Dee. I didn't mean to make you worry. How are you?

How's Laura?"

"She's fine. She's still here. She helps me here when she can. Right now she's over at the Home."

"What's the Home?"

"It's the old Community Center, over by the Fire Department. It's where orphaned children and the elderly live now."

"That's good. I'm glad she's okay. And Nora?" Jane followed Dee out the back door.

"Nora's still here too. She just turned ten. She's got a sister now, too."

"No way. Really?"

"Yup. Baby Grace is ten months old now. The most beautiful baby you've ever seen."

"I'll go there after I leave here. I can't wait to see Laura again. So the Farmer's Market is now a restaurant?"

"Yeah. After a year or two, we started getting busy up here again, with people crossing the mountains. Laura thought it would be a good idea to have a place for people to gather. Since she already had experience in food service, and the Market was so close to the intersection, it just seemed right. It was all Laura's idea; I'm not real sure how I ended up running it. You worked with Laura. You know how she is."

"Probably because she's bit off more than she can chew. Again."

Momma Dee laughed. "You're absolutely right. God bless Laura, but she always has tried to do more than she can handle. It's the same confidence that possessed her to take all those advanced classes in school. By the time exams rolled around, she hadn't seen daylight in two weeks." Dee laughed shook her head. "I don't know where she gets it."

"So where is everybody?" Jane changed the subject. "Who are all those people in there?"

"Some of them are just passing through. Most of them are citizens. They live here," Dee said.

"What happened to all the people who used to live here? I don't recognize hardly any of the people in there."

"A lot has changed since you've been gone, Jane. Most of the people who used to live here are dead. Some from natural causes, a few from accidents. Don Barkley fell from a roof he was trying to fix. Died from an aneurysm two days later."

Jane remembered Don. He was a kind man with an easy laugh. He had a landscaping company and mowed her grass every Wednesday. Jane shook a couple of cigarettes out of her pack and handed one to Dee.

"The hardest ones were the ones who died from causes that used to be preventable. You'd be surprised how many people had diabetes." Dee went quiet for a moment. "All those people had been happy and healthy before, with modern medicine. It was so hard to watch them wither away without it."

"I'm sorry I wasn't around, Dee."

"There's nothing you could've done." She took a long draw from the cigarette. "But that's in the past. We've got more important things to worry about now."

"I assume you're talking about the National Guard?"

"I had a bad feeling about them the moment they came to town. Everything was going really well until they showed up."

"What about the bodies hanging from the street lights? One of them is just a boy, Dee!"

Dee aged ten years when Jane asked that question.

"I know, hun. The hangings are a relatively recent development. The powers that be decided that we apparently have too much freedom in this town. They introduced a whole slew of new laws, outlawing many things that were completely harmless. The boy just got caught between a rock and a hard place." Momma Dee looked at the boy's body hanging in the distance,

"It was just him and his momma. She got sick and couldn't work. They made a law requiring all kids under sixteen to go to school. Won't even allow parents to home school their kids. Since he was havin' to go to school, he couldn't work as much. Less work meant less money meant less food. I caught him digging through my dumpster for something to eat. I was gonna give him a couple of loaves of bread, but a Guard came around the corner and saw him. Hauled him off for theft. Strung him up right then and there in front of God and everybody."

Jane could hear the bitterness dripping from every word. Tears welled up in Dee's eyes, but she didn't let them fall.

"They hung him for that? Digging through a dumpster?" Jane refused to believe it.

"Not just that. It wasn't the first time he'd been caught stealing. They use the 'three strike' rule."

"But surely they knew. They had to know about his situation—"

"Doesn't matter. Zero tolerance." She paused. "He was just hungry," she whispered, more to herself than to Jane. She took a deep breath and gathered herself. "I'm sorry, sweetie. It's just been hard lately."

Jane wrapped her arms around Dee and hugged her tight. Dee returned the gesture. Just then, a young woman came through the back door.

"There you are. I've been looking for you. They need you back inside." Her eyes widened when she noticed Jane. "Oh my God. Jane! I can't believe it."

Jane hugged her. "It's good to see you, Laura. I can't believe you had another baby."

Laura turned around to show Jane the little girl in the baby carrier on her back. The baby gurgled and stuffed her fingers in her mouth. Jane tickled her tiny toes. The baby squealed in delight and kicked her fat little legs.

"It's the only way to keep an eye on her while I'm working. In this world, I'm too nervous to leave her with someone else. It kills me that Nora has to go to school."

"How do you know if she's asleep or not?"

Laura pulled a homemade baby snack out of her pocket and held it over her shoulder. A tiny hand reached up and took it. Jane and Laura laughed.

"How's your husband doing?"

"He's good. Almost lost him to pneumonia last winter. Thank God he pulled through. He's on the construction crew now. They're building more houses closer to the intersection."

"It's just not practical to be so spread out like we used to be."

"Dee told me you're running an orphanage now?"

"Oh yes. You have to come see." Laura turned Momma Dee. "Are you okay here?"

"Oh yeah. You two go on."

Laura hugged her mother and led Jane to the other side of town.

Chapter Thirteen

There was a light knock on the door almost too soft to hear.
"What time is it?" Willa yawned.
Jane fumbled for her watch on the night stand. "Two a.m."
"Who the hell is knocking at two o'clock in the morning?" Willa climbed out of bed and went downstairs to open the door. Jane followed.

A cold, sharp breeze blew through the door. A layer of frost covered the ground and glittered in the pale moonlight. A slight figure stood in the doorway. Their jacket hood was pulled up over their head, but wisps of red hair stuck out. The visitor glanced back over her shoulder, pulling her hood further down over her eyes.

"Charlie?"

Charlie shushed her and pushed her way inside. She pushed back her hood, releasing her wild, copper curls.

"What the hell are you doing here?" Willa was shocked.

"I'm sorry for coming so late, but I had to check on Duke."

"Why?" Willa was suspicious.

"I know you don't know me well enough to trust me, but please believe me when I say I am so very sorry I had to turn you away at the clinic. It was not my choice. My superiors have the final say on who we treat. I truly wanted to help him. I did." The guilt was painted all over her face.

"See?" Jane said. "Told you so."

Willa scowled at her sister, but backed down.

"Can—can I see him?"

Jane pointed to Duke's door. Charlie let herself in. Duke was asleep on his back, one hand on his chest, one knee sticking out. A massive white dog laid curled up on the bed at his feet. The dog lifted its head and looked at her. Duke's head was turned to one side, and he snored softly. She sat down next to him and ran her hand through his sweat dampened hair. She grazed her fingers across the gauze covering his healing shoulder. Duke tossed his head and winced in his sleep.

She was terrified of being caught here, but she was so intrigued by this man who had come into the clinic half-dead just days before. It broke her heart to have to tell his sisters that she couldn't help him. She had already risked her freedom to sneak out the antibiotics for him. If she was caught fraternizing with civilians on top of that, she would be hanged.

But this man just captivated her.

Duke floated back up through the haze of his delirium. His eyes fluttered open. He struggled to bring her into focus but when he did, he just stared at her.

"Goddamn you're pretty," he breathed.

Charlie blushed and smiled.

"How are you feeling?" she asked

"I'm—I'm good. Are—" he paused, struggling to find the rest of his sentence. "Are you my reaper?"

She pursed her lips to keep from giggling. "No. You're going to be just fine."

"Damn..." He sounded disappointed.

He sighed and closed his eyes. And just like that, he was asleep again.

Charlie pushed back the bandage to look at his wound. It looked so much better than it did when he first came to her. But that didn't matter. The infection was in his blood now. There wasn't anything she or anyone else could do. She stood and walked out of the room. She didn't allow herself to stop and have one last look. Jane and

Willa were in the living room waiting for her.

"Thank you for coming," Jane said. "I understand how dangerous it is for you."

"And thank you for the antibiotics. You saved his life," Willa said.

"Don't thank me yet. He's not out of the woods. He's conscious and somewhat lucid, but he's still weak. Just keep trying to keep him fed and hydrated. Other than that, all you can do is pray. I can't offer much more advice than that."

"We understand," Jane said.

"We also know that you didn't come here at two in the morning just to check on him." Willa gave her a sly, knowing smile.

Charlie blushed again. "Anyway, I really should be going."

She pulled her hood back up and slipped back out into the night.

There was only a week's worth of antibiotics, but after that week Duke was almost completely recovered. He was still weak but had regained his appetite and began attempting to get up and move around. Jane and Willa had a hard time keeping him off his feet.

That Saturday, Jane was startled by a loud crash coming from Duke's room. She rolled her eyes and sighed. Duke had made another attempt to get up. Jane went to his room and found him in a heap in the floor, the collapsed remains of the wash table and its porcelain basin around him.

"I'm not sure what you were trying to do," she said, "but you appear to have miscalculated."

Duke groaned and pushed himself back up on his elbows. "Oh kiss my ass. My math was fine. It's not my fault that *somebody* moved the table."

"We moved it out of the way so you wouldn't knock it over."

"Well, then you're the one who miscalculated. Not me."

Jane rolled her eyes again before helping him to his feet. Though his shoulder was nearly healed, it still pained him. She took care not to pull on it too hard. He sat on the bed while Jane cleaned up the pieces of the basin.

"I just wanted to wash my damned face. I feel disgusting." He rubbed his face.

"You are disgusting. I'll go see if I can find you a basin that's a little more durable."

Jane took the broken basin and went in search of Maria. The woman had been a godsend while Jane and Willa tended to Duke. She made sure they had food, clean clothes, and linens. She even helped watch over Duke so they would have a chance to tend to their own needs. Jane was convinced that Maria was part of the reason why he survived.

Jane found Maria in the front office talking to a Guard. His insignia said he was a Master Sergeant. He ignored her as she walked in with the remains of the basin. It was the same guy from the processing center. Sergeant Smith. He was a couple of inches shorter than Jane. His slim frame was nearly swallowed whole by his baggy uniform. Nonetheless, he had the carriage and demeanor of a man who demanded, and usually received, respect that he hadn't earned. Jane was wary of him. Something about him, his demeanor, felt domineering and foreboding.

"What you are doing here is illegal. I am being generous by giving you the opportunity to cease your operation before punitive action is taken."

"What? Renting rooms? It's an inn! How is renting rooms illegal?"

"You're not just renting rooms. Don't lie to me. You're prostituting those women, and they are taking my Guards as their clients! This type of activity is illegal, and it will not be tolerated in Cashiers Village."

"I don't know where you get your information, but I am not pimping those girls out. The only money I get from my tenants is rent payments. What they do in their rooms is their own business.

I have no control over it."

"But you are aware of their activities. You are guilty by association."

"Guilty of what? You have no proof of anything or you would've searched the rooms by now. All you have is rumors and speculation. According to the old laws and yours, you have nothing to accuse me of."

He stared her down. He knew she was right, but lack of evidence hadn't stopped him before.

"We're not through," he snapped. Only when he turned to leave did he notice Jane.

"I'm so sorry, Maria. It was an accident." Jane handed the basin to her.

"It's okay, amiga. Sergeant Smith was—"

"I'm looking for Duke Campbell," Sergeant Smith interrupted, moving on to the next thing on his to do list.

"Excuse you," Jane said disbelieving. This guy was an asshole. "That was rude."

Smith ignored her. "You are his sister, correct?"

"Are you not going to apologize?" Jane ignored his question in turn.

"For what?"

"For being rude. Maria was speaking to me and you interrupted her. It's rude to interrupt." Her heartbeat revved, but she didn't back down.

Smith stared at her. "Are you lecturing me?"

"I'm not lecturing anyone. You were rude and you should apologize."

"Where is Duke Campbell?" he barked.

"I am not going to accommodate someone who has no manners. Either apologize or find him yourself."

Maria didn't say a word during their exchange. Jane saw her cross herself out of the corner of her eye. Maria shook her head imperceptibly, warning Jane not to goad this man. Her heart hammered against her chest. It was like facing down Emory all over again but much worse. Then, she was reasonably sure that Emory wasn't a real threat. Smith, on the other hand, was a very real, very present threat.

She crossed her arms across her chest to keep herself from trembling. She and Willa had laid low for the past few weeks, but it seemed that the time had come to make an impression and damned if Jane's first impression was going to be a trembling coward. It was a struggle, but Jane kept her expression deadpan and uninterested.

A vein throbbed in his temple and his jaw twitched as he ground his teeth. Smith all but growled at her. Jane decided not to push her luck. She rolled her eyes and headed toward the door.

"I'll be right back, Maria."

She walked out of the office and headed back to the cabin. Smith whistled. Jane turned to see several more Guards join them from the street.

"Woah, woah, woah. Hold up. What the hell is this?"

"They're here to assist, should the situation become hostile."

"If the situation becomes hostile, it'll be your fault."

"And why is that?"

"Because you're rude. And overbearing. And an asshole."

She started to open the door, but Smith pushed her out of the way and beat on the door with his fist. His cronies fanned out behind him.

"Open the door, Campbell, by order of the Governor!"

Less than five seconds passed before he beat on the door again. "Open up, Campbell. NOW!"

"For Christ's sake, let him get to the door. He's still recovering."

Smith backhanded her, knocking her to the floor.

"You need to learn to shut your mouth." He raised his hand again to bang on the door, but it swung open.

Duke stood in the doorway in nothing but his boxers. His mountainous frame towered over Smith, forcing him to crane his neck to look up at Duke. Even recovering from a near death experience, and wearing only his underwear, Duke was formidable. Nuke poked his head out the door by Duke's knee. He growled at Sergeant Smith.

Duke glanced down at Jane, still on the floor, a bruise beginning to blossom around her eye. The look of confusion on Dukes face faded to anger.

"Why is my sister on the floor?" His voice was calm, but only just. Jane could see the anger simmering beneath the thin veil of composure.

Smith was once again lost for words, but this time out of shear fear. It was like watching Barney Fife stare down the Incredible Hulk.

Smith ignored him. "I am here to take you to the processing center. You are required to submit to a search and interrogation upon entering the Village. You were, unfortunately, incapable of answering questions upon your arrival. Since you have recovered—"

"No thanks to ya'll," Duke rumbled.

Duke pushed past Smith and pulled Jane to her feet. He prodded her chin, turning her face so he could see the purple shadow darkening her cheekbone.

"You okay?"

Jane nodded.

"Where's Willa?"

"I dunno. I think she's at the Fire Station."

He nodded and glanced out to Sergeant Smith and his welcoming committee.

"Don't do anything stupid," she whispered.

The corner of his mouth twitched up in an impish little smile, his eyes crinkling. He winked.

She gave him a confused look but went inside.

"Now that you have recovered you are required to submit yourself to questioning."

Duke turned to go back inside.

Smith pulled a gun and aimed it at Duke. Several other barrels raised behind him. Jane's heart lodged in her throat where it continued to hammer out a frantic beat.

"Don't make me ask you again. You're already walking a thin line," Smith warned.

Duke turned again, stopped and seemed to consider something. He shrugged and walked out on the porch. He slid his feet into his boots without lacing them up.

"Okay, Gomer. Let's go."

Smith looked at him confused. He lowered his gun, but kept it trained on Duke.

"Are you not going to put on clothes?"

"Well, I was going to, but seeing as how you threatened to shoot me if I went back inside." He shrugged. "I figured I'd spent enough time recovering from injuries. No need for both of us to be laid up."

"What exactly is that supposed to mean?"

"It means if you'd shot me, you would've dearly wished you hadn't."

"Is that a threat?" Smith's eyes bugged out of his head in rage. The vein in his temple began to pulse again.

"If that's the way you want to interpret it, there's not much I can do to change your mind."

Duke strode across the yard with all of the invincible confidence of a man who had just come back from the dead. Smith and his entourage just stood there, dumbstruck. When he realized he was alone, Duke turned back.

"Ya'll need to hurry up. I ain't got no idea where I'm going, and I can only stroll away confidently for so far before I look like an idiot."

Chapter Fourteen

"State your name for the record."

"Benjamin Matthew Campbell." Still in his boxers, Duke leaned his chair back on two legs, put his huge, filthy boots on the table and put his hands behind his head. He watched the Guard across the table with an amused grin.

"And your alias is 'Duke,' correct?"

"That is correct."

"How did you come by that nickname?"

"Didn't ya'll confiscate my stuff when we got here?"

"Yes..."

"Then I assume you saw the gunpowder, the tannerite, and the fireworks?"

"Yes, and we will get to that, but what does that have to do with my question?"

Duke let his chair fall back on all four legs with a bang. He feigned a look of hurt and disbelief.

"Oh c'mon. You were alive before the Crash. Don't tell me you've never heard of Duke Nukem."

"I see."

The guard made a note on his clipboard. Duke rolled his eyes.

"And where are you from originally?"

"Seriously, dude? You went through my shit weeks ago. And you interrogated my sisters already. You know the answer to all of these questions. My name is Benjamin Matthew Campbell. Everybody calls me Duke. My sisters are Jane and Willa. We are from South

Carolina, just across the state line from here. Jane lived here in Cashiers Village. A year after the Crash, we left and traveled around. We've been gone for three years and now we're back." Duke was starting to get irritated.

The Guard had the good grace to look a little sheepish. "My apologies. I'm just doing my job." He shifted through his notes. "There are just a few routine questions that we ask in every citizenship interview. You have already gone through the medical exam and interview. This is more of a personal interview. To see who you are as a person, to see if you would be more of an asset or a liability."

"Well that certainly is a change of tune. When I got here, I was immediately written off as a liability."

"And what makes you say that?" The Guard's tone was gently encouraging, like a psychiatrist probing for more detailed answers.

"Well, I guess it would be the fact that your people refused me treatment and left me to die. I must say, that first impression does little to endear me to you or the government you represent."

"You must understand, we have limited supplies here. What we have must be saved for those who are more likely to live and be productive members of society. I think, considering the circumstances, we were more than generous in letting you stay with your sisters and allowing them to provide your care."

"Oh yes, very generous to allow me to die in the relative comfort of a small cabin, surrounded by family. You make it sound like I was treated like a king."

"Well, the usual policy for someone who has been denied citizenship is to escort them to the edge of town and send them on their way."

"Even if they're on their deathbed?"

"It's not common, but I won't lie and say that hasn't happened. Like I said, resources are limited and we're not going to waste them on people who cannot contribute."

"You're kidding me."

"No, I am not. Shall we continue?"

Duke shook his head. "Jesus Christ," he whispered under his breath. "Yeah. I guess. What else you wanna know?"

"What did you do for a living before the Crash?"

"Nothing. I'd just gotten out of college. I didn't have a chance to start anything before the world ended…"

"What were your hobbies?"

"Video games, mostly. And football. But I dabbled in blacksmithing and weapon making. Knives, short swords, that sort of thing."

"Tell me about the gunpowder, fireworks, and tannerite you had in your belongings when you arrived."

"This doesn't sound like a 'routine' question."

"Well it is routine, when an intimidating man shows up in town with explosives, to find out just what the hell he was doing."

"Fair enough," Duke ceded to the Guard. "When Jane, Willa, and I left the Village, we kind of felt like it was a chance for us to do whatever we wanted. We didn't have jobs anymore to tie us down. We could go anywhere. Do anything. So I decided to explore my longtime interest in explosives."

"And why exactly are you interested in explosives?"

Duke raised an eyebrow. "I'm an adult male living in the rural south, in redneck country. We have an innate interest in blowing shit up."

"How did you make a living? By that I mean, what means did you use to survive?"

"If we came across a town or settlement, we would trade work for food and shelter. Otherwise, we just knew how to do shit. I know how to hunt. Jane knows first aid stuff. Willa knows how to cook. We got by."

"What about supplies? You had many things in your inventory like batteries and coffee that you obviously didn't make yourself."

"We scavenged a lot. If we found a house or something, we

would stake it out, see if anyone lived there."

"And if they did?"

"We left them alone."

"Why?"

"Willa asked the same question a thousand times, but I agreed with Jane. We wouldn't want people to steal from us, so why would we steal from them? She always said it was up to us to shape the new world we live in. So if someone had already claimed something, we left it alone. If not, we took it."

"What would you take? Were you looking for anything in particular?"

"Not really. Anything of value. We used what we needed and saved the rest for trading. Willa has a real knack for finding the good stuff."

"How so?"

"I dunno. She just knows all the best places to find stuff. She would find local maps and figure out where the high-end neighborhoods were. And places that people wouldn't think to look. We found a nice stash of first aid supplies at an aquarium once. I wouldn't have thought of it."

The Guard made a note on his clipboard.

"The last question is something we'd all like to know. How did you manage to travel through Blue Valley territory without a scratch?"

"And I will respond with the same thing I've already said several times. You already know the answer from Jane's and Willa's interrogations."

"Interview."

"No. This is an interrogation. I'll tell you why." He leaned forward, elbows on the table, a finger in the Guard's face. "You're asking us all the same questions. You don't believe us. You're trying to find out if our stories line up. You think we're lying. Hell if I know why. What do we have to lie about?

"But I'll answer your question the same way I'm sure both of them did. Jane knew Nolan from before the Crash. He was one of her regulars at the restaurant she worked at. After the Crash, Nolan left and established the Blue Valley Boys and Jane helped orchestrate a peaceful trade agreement between them and Cashiers Village."

"When you say Jane knows Nolan, what is the nature of their relationship? Are they acquaintances, or would you say they're friends?"

"They're friends, yes. Jane was his bookkeeper." Duke didn't like the sound of that question, even less than all the others.

"I thought she was a waitress."

"Well, it is technically feasible for a person to have two jobs."

"Thank you for being honest with me. There is an opening at the forge. They need a blacksmith. A man as strong as you are, or will be when you recover, would make a good blacksmith. I strongly suggest talking to Tony." He wrote down an address and handed it to Duke. "Please consider the next few days as a vacation of sorts. After being confined for your recovery, I'm sure you will appreciate being able to get out and about. You are free to enjoy what the Village has to offer, without responsibility, for the next three days. Afterward, you are expected to earn your place in the Village."

He scrawled out a spiky signature on one of the papers on his clipboard. He pulled a stamp out of a pocket and stamped the paper next to his signature. He handed the paper to Duke. "Keep this on your person at all times. It explains your citizenship and the fact that you have yet to find employment. If anyone asks, just show them this. You will receive more permanent identification once you find employment."

Duke scanned the paper. It had only a few short lines outlining his situation, the signature, and the stamp. He folded it up and started to put it in his pocket until he remembered he wasn't wearing pants. The Guard extended his hand. Duke stood and shook it. The Guard seemed a little disconcerted that he was nearly naked.

"Welcome to Cashiers Village, Mr. Campbell," he said. He opened the door and held it for Duke.

"Thanks," Duke said, and left. He walked outside. He squinted and held his hand up to his eyes, blinded by the bright sunlight. He strode down the street back to the cabin. Jane and Willa stood up when he walked in. There was an air of concern as the three of them stood there looking at each other; Jane dressed for riding, Willa in a t-shirt, a pair of cotton shorts, and sneakers, and Duke in just his boxers and untied boots.

Willa collapsed on the couch in side splitting laughter. When Duke joined in, Jane sighed and unfolded her arms. The tension that had been building in her neck finally released.

Duke excused himself and went to his room. He returned wearing a pair of jeans and a shirt, holding a pair of socks in his hand. He sat down on the couch.

"Okay," he said, pulling on his socks. His face twisted as he strained to reach his feet. "So, we have officially been accepted as citizens of a town we were already citizens of to begin with. I'll probably be working at the blacksmith shop. What is today?"

"Friday."

"Oh, cool. So, what have I missed?"

"Well, they 'suggested' I work at the stables," said Willa, "but I'm not shoveling horse shit so I told them to shove that up their ass."

"How did that go?"

"She almost got her ass beat. But she ran into a group of Searchers and they found out she's pretty good at finding stuff, so…"

"Neat. What the hell is that?"

"They go out into outlying areas to look for supplies. They've found pretty much all there is to find around here so now they've started dealing with trading with other groups."

"What about you, Jane?"

"I'm gonna work at the restaurant across the street. The Farmer's Market. Momma Dee looks like she needs help."

"They told me to talk to some guy named Tony at the blacksmith shop. So, are we not going back to Blue Valley?"

It had been their custom that, when the first frost fell, they would find the nearest town or settlement and stay there through the winter.

"Might as well stay here. It's as good a place as any," Jane said.

"Even with the Guard running the show?" Willa asked.

"It won't last," Duke said. "Guys like that, they never do. They build their power up like that until it collapses in on itself, or until somebody tears it down."

Another knock on the door.

"For the love of God, what now?" Willa snapped.

It was Maria with the new wash basin. Willa flushed red.

"Sorry, Maria. Just a little on edge."

"It's okay." She sounded sad.

Maria took a deep shuddering breath and steadied her shaking voice. Duke took the basin to his room while Maria sat down.

"So what was Smith talking about, Maria? Something about prostitutes?" Jane asked.

Willa and Duke looked at them in confusion and shock.

"What are ya'll talking about?" Willa asked.

"When I took the broken basin to Maria, Smith was in the office accusing Maria of pimping out prostitutes."

Duke threw his head back and laughed heartily. He didn't know Maria very well, but he knew her well enough to know that the very idea was ludicrous.

Maria rolled her eyes. "No, I'm not pimping out prostitutes. But they do live here. There's always been two or three girls in town willing to lay on their backs for a few bucks. Mostly, they took advantage of the travelers coming through town. But in the past year or so, there's been more and more."

"But why do they live here of all places? You'd think they'd find a place a little more inconspicuous," Willa said.

"Well, most of them are doing it because they're desperate. It's the only way they can afford to eat. They have their regulars. But the regulars can be, well, they can be rough."

"You mean they beat them." There was a low, angry edge to his voice.

Maria nodded. "I found one of them behind a vegetable patch one night. Broken nose. Black eyes. It was raining and I couldn't just leave her out there. So I brought her back, tended to her, and gave her a room. I guess word spread because I have about fifteen of them living here now."

"How do you get away with that? The Guard has obviously caught on," Jane said.

"They work for me. No, literally," she added at their shocked expressions. "They work for the inn. They do housekeeping, tend to the garden, run the front desk. I just wanted to make sure they had a safe place to live. Like I told Smith, what they do in their rooms is their business. Though, I guess I'll have to get them to stop that. The last thing I need is a raid."

Duke walked over and squatted down in front of her. He took her tiny hands into his large ones and looked her in the eye.

"Listen to me, Maria. As long as I'm around, nothing and no one is going to hurt you or the girls. I promise."

She nodded, her chin trembling.

"Don't worry about us," Willa chimed in. "We'll be fine."

Willa turned to Jane. "Well, we've got the weekend off. What do we do now?"

"I want to go home," Jane said.

Chapter Fifteen

"Everything looks like it's in order here," the Guard said. They said they had come to do the safety inspection ("because nothing is more important than the safety of our citizens"), but Jane wasn't fooled. They were looking for weapons and supplies. The Guard gave Jane yet another piece of paper with a signature and a stamp.

They had come back to Jane's house on the edge of town. The home she had once shared with her husband. The little house was barely a thousand square feet, situated at the top of a steep gravel lane on the side of a mountain. A tiny square of yard, a narrow driveway, and a garage tucked up next to a steep twenty-foot bank. It wasn't much, but it was her home. Until now, she hadn't realized how much she had missed it: her husband, the comfort.

"Pompous little prick," Willa muttered as soon as the Guard was out of earshot.

Jane waited and watched until he was well and gone. As soon as she heard the horse's hooves on the street below, she turned to them and said, "Come on."

She led them across the small yard to the shed on the other side of the driveway. Jane fished a ring of keys out of her pocket and unlocked the padlock. She left the door wide open to see. Her little silver Honda was still here under an inch of dust. The left wall was always her little corner. All of her gardening tools and fertilizers were piled on the shelves, an array of baskets shoved unceremoniously underneath. She could almost hear Levi, his exasperated voice begging her to please put the box of Christmas decorations away.

"C'mon now, it's April." It was a stark contrast to the back wall. The shelves were full of tools, oil cans, and power equipment. But unlike Jane's erratic mess, there was a systematic order to the back shelves. Each tool had its own place; lawn equipment up top, power tools on the shelf above the tool box. And on top of the tool box, several tool batteries sitting in their chargers.

Jane's chest tightened. It had been two years since Levi had died. The pain had never really gone away. She just got better at hiding it. Willa and Duke were always there to remind her that it hadn't been her fault, but she would never forgive herself. She took a deep breath and pushed the hard lump of guilt back down.

She found a flashlight and led them to a large metal cabinet standing against the back wall.

"There's nothing in there, Jane, the guy just searched it," Willa said.

"I am aware of that. I am also aware of something he was not." Jane grinned and pulled the cabinet back away from the wall. It was only then that Willa and Duke noticed that the cabinet was on wheels and rolled away easily.

"Woah," Willa and Duke chorused.

Behind the cabinet, set into the wall, was a door. Jane unlocked two more padlocks and opened the door. A musty, earthy scent escaped from the darkness. Jane clicked on the flashlight and walked into the darkness.

"WOAH!" they said again. In the narrow beam of the flashlight they saw a small stash of rifles, handguns, ammunition, knives, machetes, and many other weapons, not to mention boxes of emergency rations and several dozen bottles of wine. Nuke started his cursory sniff around the edge of the cellar.

"Levi built me this root cellar years ago. We thought we were being clever, building it behind the garage, but when the world went to shit, it turned out to be a good hiding place."

"Why didn't you tell us about this?" Willa picked up a set of hot pink brass knuckles.

"The less you knew, the less you could say under interrogation."

"Good point."

"It's good to know we've got something to replace what they confiscated," Duke said. Most of their belongings had been "taken for the betterment of the community."

"I can understand the guns and the bow, but our knives? Really? A knife is more of a tool than a weapon." Willa was still seething over that.

"Yeah, but their goal is complete control. You can't control people who can fight for themselves. And they can't fight for themselves without weapons," Duke said.

Willa picked up a green, aluminum baseball bat and swung it a couple of times. "But why, though? Why do they want that much control?"

"Why not? Why did the Romans expand their empire? Why did the British Empire try to colonize everything? Because they can. Because they're powerful and they have the means to make anyone do anything they want." Duke scratched his beard.

"Control the people, control the resources," Jane supplied.

"Exactly. But why Cashiers Village?" Duke picked up a slingshot and started playing with it.

"It's one of the few safe places left to cross the mountains. Thousands of people came through Cashiers Village every year," Jane said. "It's not a major city like Asheville, but people still knew about it. That was one of the big things the council made a point to maintain, a safe place for people to come. They knew people would be trying to cross the mountains to find their families. The least we could do was give them a safe place to do it, unlike the big cities. You remember what Knoxville was like."

Willa nodded. "I've never been that scared in my life. I honestly thought we were going to die in that hell hole."

"And most people will come through Cashiers Village trying to avoid places like that."

"We were the only ones dumb enough to actually go there." Duke held the sling shot up at eye level. He put his thumb in the pocket and pushed it away from him, stretching the rubber straps as far as his arm would reach.

"I have a bad feeling about these National Guard people." Willa folded her arms and leaned against the block wall.

"Yeah, me too. I worry about the people they're letting in. They only let us in cause we're locals. I'm almost positive they wouldn't have let us in if we weren't."

"Yeah, we didn't make a very good first impression. Duke, will you stop dicking around?" Willa admonished.

"I'm trying to see how far I can stretch this."

Willa rolled her eyes. "You think they're only letting in people that agree with them?"

"Exactly. If you're trying to gain control over a society, would you fill it with people that didn't like what you were doing?"

"Nope."

"Ow, damn it." Duke's thumb slipped. The slingshot had snapped back and smacked him in the face.

Jane laughed. Duke rubbed his eye with the heel of his hand.

"Dude, will you act your age?" Willa asked.

"I don't know how to act my age. I've never been this age before. But I have been twelve before. I know how to act like that."

Chapter Sixteen

As it was harvest season, Duke spent the next three weeks working in the fields. The entire town was hard at work preserving the harvest for the coming winter. Surplus crops were divided among the citizens, albeit unevenly. It was clear that some people received more than others. It was also clear that those people were the new citizens and not the locals.

There was a harvest festival the last week of October. Willa organized a special search trip to a year-round Halloween store in Georgia to find costumes for the kids. Momma Dee had several people working around the clock making candy so the kids could go trick-or-treating. Every building was decked out with pumpkins, cornstalks, and jewel-colored ears of corn. Copper-colored leaves swirled through the streets.

The festival ended with a rodeo staged on the baseball field by the Rec Department. A large arena had been erected, with large overhead lights mounted on twenty-foot poles at each corner. The ground had been covered in a layer of sand. People packed into the bleachers on both sides. The air was thick with the scent of popcorn and barn animals.

Somehow, Jane found herself at the back of the arena, near the chutes, holding Mahz's reins. She tried to remember how Willa and Duke had managed to convince her to compete in the barrel racing competition, but her anxiety was blocking out all thought. She had already watched three women go out and race around the barrels, their times averaging around eighteen seconds.

She took a few deep breaths. This little arena was nothing. She had spent countless hours racing around whatever they could find with Mahz, competing against Willa and her grey Mustang, Eleanor. Eleanor was fast, but Mahz was so nimble he could turn on a dime. Granted, Jane had found him at a farm that trained barrel horses, but Mahz just seemed to have it in his blood.

Willa walked up to her, fingers in the pockets of her jeans. She smiled at Jane.

"Have you seen Duke?" she asked.

"He's over there with his buddies."

Duke was sitting high up in the bleachers on the left side of the arena with Carlos and Darin. The three of them seemed to be getting along famously. There was a gaggle of girls at the bottom of the bleachers. They kept looking up at Duke, then turning back to each other and giggling. Duke kept looking down at them flirting, grinning, and winking. He also kept looking out at the stands across the arena from him, staring at someone. Willa couldn't make out who it was. She turned back to Jane.

"You ready for this?"

"Don't have much of a choice, do I?"

"You got this." She noticed how hard Jane's hands were trembling. Her voice softened. "Look, you don't have to do this if you don't want to. I was just thinking it might be fun."

"Why don't you do it?"

"Mahz doesn't respond to me like he does to you. And Eleanor gets too jumpy around loud crowds."

The racer slated to ride before Jane led her horse up to the chutes. She looked Jane up and down and sneered. She was unattractively thin and had dark eyebrows. She tucked her long, blonde hair behind her ear and settled her hat on her head. She looked over Mahz and his worn tack and rolled her eyes.

Jane didn't recognize her. She must have been a new citizen. Even now, the stark white and silver threads in her blue plaid shirt glittered in the spotlight. She smelled like starch, perfume, and new leather. Her horse's saddle seemed to gleam in the overhead light. She had the clothes and carriage of someone from a wealthy and influential family, but her looks were rather plain and haughty. It was a sharp contrast to Jane and Willa's worn and faded jeans.

"You got something you wanna say?" Willa asked.

"No, no. Just...good luck. You're gonna need it."

"Is that supposed to mean something?" Willa's brow furrowed.

"Willa, let it go," Jane whispered.

Willa ignored her. "If I'm not mistaken, it kinda sounds like you're trying to start shit."

"Oh no, not at all. All I'm saying is it doesn't look like you've done this a whole lot. I've been barrel racing since I was nine. You might want to save yourself the embarrassment."

"Let me guess, Mommy and Daddy paid for you to have lessons, bought you everything you ever wanted, and didn't even watch you use it."

"Is that supposed to mean something?" the woman echoed Willa.

"Oh no, not at all. All I'm saying is it looks like you were raised by a nanny and bottle fed your superiority."

"Excuse me?" The woman seemed shocked that someone dared speak to her that way.

"Go screw yourself, Malibu Barbie." Willa turned back to Jane. "I take back what I said. You have to compete. You have to whip that bitch's ass."

The announcer came over the loud speaker. "Next up is Jennifer Smith. She's new here in town so let's give her some love!"

The crowd cheered as the blonde lined up her quarter horse and waited for her signal.

"How are they powering this place anyway?" Willa asked. A short blast from an air horn and Jennifer was off.

"Generators."

"Where'd they get the gas, though? We stopped finding viable gasoline two years ago. It all went bad."

"Propane." Jane smiled as she remembered what Levi had told her. "You can convert engines to run on propane. It's cleaner and has an indefinite shelf life. A lot of homes up here ran their heat on propane, so there's hundreds of tanks of propane just waiting to be tapped."

"I'm surprised they allowed any fuel to be used for this. They're so stingy with resources. This seems like a waste," Willa said.

Jennifer rounded the first two barrels and headed for the third.

"Yeah, but you've got to keep morale up. Nobody starts a riot faster than bored, angry citizens."

Jennifer came flying back down the arena and through the chutes.

"Bread and circuses."

"Yup."

"Nineteen point six-nine. Not a bad time. Good job, Jennifer!" the announcer called.

"You're up."

Jane swung her leg over Mahz and settled into the saddle. She gathered the reins in her hand and turned him around. Mahz pricked his ears forward and turned to look at the chutes. He knew what was coming. He tried to walk toward them but Jane held him back.

"Take it easy, buddy. I know you're excited."

"Good luck," Willa called. She had climbed up on the rails to get a good view.

"Yeah, good luck." Jennifer leered from behind her.

Jane turned and scowled at her. She looked back at Willa. *You know what? I'll show her. Come here.*

"Lift up," she said to Mahz and tugged on the reins a little. Mahz lifted his head. Jane reached up and unclasped the bridle from around his chin and pulled the headstall off. Mahz obliged and spit out the bit. Willa ran forward with a wide grin and took the bridle.

"For real? You're gonna do this without it?"

"We did it a lot when his old bridle broke, remember? It took a while to find another good one."

Willa nodded. She couldn't stop grinning. She ran back to the rails to get a good spot. Duke saw her getting lined up. He stood up and whooped and hollered.

"Our next rider is Jane Campbell and her trusty steed, Maserati. Let's hope he's as fast as his name implies. What's this? It looks like Jane is going to ride sans bridle. It's a risky move, as most horses are trained to take commands from the rider with the reins. Let's just hope she doesn't come to regret this decision."

Jane patted Mahz's neck. Mahz snorted and danced on the spot, itching to take off.

"We got this. You remember how to take cues without a bit. It's all in the knees." She nudged him with her knees to show him that's how she would be giving cues. She wound her fingers into his mane and lined up at the chutes. She glanced over and saw Jennifer. The smug grin had been replaced with a sour grimace. She backed Mahz up enough to get a running start.

At the sound of the air horn, Jane dug her heels into Mahz's side.

"Hup, hup, hup!" she called.

He leaped forward and began to build momentum. The wind blew her hair back from her face and an exhilarating thrill burned through her chest. The burst of speed didn't last long, though. As they entered the arena, Jane tugged on his mane and nudged him as they prepared to turn around the first barrel. She pushed one hand against the saddle horn, the other still wound up in his mane. She sat back in the saddle and shifted her weight. Mahz leaned in deep and danced around the barrel.

A few seconds later they repeated it around the second barrel. The roar of the crowd fell away. All she could hear was the creaking of the saddle, the jingling of hardware, the rapid thunder of hooves, and Mahz's heavy, snorting breaths. As they pulled out of the second turn, Jane looked ahead at the third and final barrel at the far end of the arena. Mahz straightened back up and took off. Jane beat out a rhythm with her heels, egging him on.

"Hup, hup, hup! Go, boy, go!"

She was out of breath and breathing hard. Mahz snorted with every breath as they tore down the arena. The third and final turn. Jane braced herself. It took every bit of her strength to sit up right. Mahz executed the turn perfectly. The thrill was back in Jane's chest. The home stretch. They had made all three turns without touching the barrels. With breath she didn't have she let out a whoop, her arms working back and forth in time with Mahz's neck.

They came back through the chutes and Jane leaned back to slow Mahz to a trot, then a walk. Mahz snorted and shook his head as he caught his breath and cooled down. She walked him around for a moment, waiting on the announcer to tell her her time.

"Seventeen point nine-one. And without a bridle! I am thoroughly impressed. Better luck next time, Jennifer."

Willa and Duke came running up to her before she had a chance to get out of the saddle. Jennifer threw her hat on the ground.

Chapter Seventeen

"I miss wi-fi. Being able to Google anything, anywhere." Everybody took a drink.

"I miss Netflix. So many hours of my life, down the drain." Everybody took a drink.

"I miss Internet porn." A moment of silence, then Duke raised his bottle to his lips, followed by Carlos and Darin.

"You guys are gross." They all laughed.

They were all sitting around the little campfire, playing a drinking game they had invented. After the rodeo had shut down, several people built campfires in the dirt behind the chutes. Many people were hanging out, drinking. One of the fires belonged to Duke and his newfound friends. Jane was still coming down off her adrenaline high, and Willa couldn't stop talking about it. "Did you see that bitch's face?"

Darin was playing tug of war with Nuke with a piece of rope. Nuke growled, but his tail bounced around like an excited feather duster. Carlos noticed Duke staring across the field at a group of people standing by one of the other fires. Carlos looked to see what Duke was staring at.

"Who is that?" Duke furrowed his brow. "I know her. How do I know her?"

"Which one?" Carlos asked.

Jane and Willa turned. They knew exactly who he was talking about.

"That's Charlie."

"No, the woman."

"Yes, the woman," Willa replied. "Her name is Charlotte. She's the nurse who saved your life."

"You mean the one who put me out on my ass and said, 'Good luck?'"

"No, the one who risked her job, and probably her life, to smuggle out the medicine you needed and said, 'Good luck.'" Willa looked at him.

"Oh."

"She also came to check on you while you were sick."

Duke remembered. It was hazy, but he recalled her vibrant red hair and her soft hands.

"I should thank her."

"You can't," Carlos said. "She's not supposed to socialize with us. She risked her job giving you the medicine. If you thanked her, you'd be admitting, not only that she gave you the medicine, but also that she came to see you. She'd be hanged. You too, probably."

"Why can't she socialize with us?" Willa was confused, but Duke understood.

"She works for the government. For them to maintain their hold on this town, they keep us in the dark. The less the populace knows, the better," Darin said.

"And what better way to prevent the spread of that knowledge than to prevent us from talking to them in the first place," Jane added.

The Campbells fell into a rhythm over the following weeks. Duke enjoyed his work at the forge. Willa, with her ingenious searching methods, helped Carlos run the search team. Jane was finally relaxed and even happy. As the weather turned colder, life in the Village slowed down. Fewer travelers came through, and people spent more and more time at home. The last week of November, the Campbells slept in. They finally got up when they heard long, loud blasts from an air horn. They dressed and went to find Maria in the office.

"They're calling a town meeting." Her expression was somber. "Nothing good has ever come out of these meetings. Come, we'll go together."

Maria led them through the park to the mowed Commons. There were already a couple hundred people there. The U-shaped stage was lined with people in uniform. A podium had been erected in the middle of the stage. People milled about for almost half an hour before someone approached the podium. The crowd, which had nearly doubled, fell silent.

"Thank you all for coming." The man was not wearing a uniform but rather a dark blue suit and tie. He looked more like a politician. "For those of you who are new here, my name is Adam King, and I am the governor of what will eventually be the collective state of Carolina. We have successfully created a thriving community here in Cashiers Village, and we hope that it will continue. Unfortunately, I am stepping down from my post here in the Village. As our state continues to grow and prosper, my expertise is needed elsewhere. I have called this meeting to formally introduce you to your new governor, Sergeant Anthony Smith."

The Campbells groaned in unison as Sergeant Smith approached the podium and shook King's hand.

"Oh this is bad," Jane whispered. "This is very bad."

"Thank you, Adam," Smith said. "And thank you, Cashiers Village, for electing me to this post—"

Willa turned to Jane. "Elected? Who the hell voted for him?"

"More importantly, when did they have an election? Maria, was there an election before we got here?"

"No. This is the first I'm hearing of any election."

"—with all due respect to my predecessor, there are a few things that will change under my jurisdiction, but rest assured, they will be minor changes and will ultimately lead to a better and more prosperous Cashiers Village."

After a grand round of applause, the crowd dispersed. Momma Dee saw Jane and came over.

"Dee, did you know about this election?"

"Unfortunately, yes. I heard several of the new people talking about it. Apparently, only those citizens chosen by the Guard to live here were allowed to vote."

"That's ridiculous. Why wouldn't they let us vote?"

"The same reason they pick and choose who they let in," Duke said. "They're controlling everything. They wanted Smith in charge. They only let people who agree with them live here and vote here. If we had been allowed to vote, Smith wouldn't have won."

Willa looked at him in awe and fascination. "You have got to stop reading those sociology books."

Duke shrugged.

The Campbells turned to walk back through the park with Maria. Before they made it to the gravel pathway, they were stopped by a Guard.

"Which one of you is Willa Campbell?"

"I am."

"You are under arrest for breaking and entering and theft. Come with us."

Two more Guards joined the first. All of them held rifles. Willa looked at Jane and Duke. All of them were bewildered.

"What the hell are you talking about? I've been here the entire time."

"You are accused of breaking into a home and stealing late last night."

"That's bullshit," Duke interjected. "She was with us all night last night. She didn't go anywhere."

"You are sentenced to three days in the labor camp. Come with us."

"No. I'm not going anywhere. I have rights!"

Two of the Guards came forward and grabbed her by her arms.

Willa kicked and fought like a cornered animal.

"Wait. She's right. You can't do this," Jane cried. "You can't sentence her without a trial. You haven't even told us what it was she stole, or who accused her!"

"No, she's not. Yes, we can. And no, we don't have to tell you anything. She will be released in three days." He turned to the Guards holding Willa. "Take her away."

Willa writhed and screamed. "Let me go you bastards. You can't do this. This is disgusting. Screw you. Screw all of you. Jane!"

"I'll figure it out, Willa," Jane called. She turned to Duke. "What are we going to do?"

"You have to go to the central office. The old gas station on the corner. That's where you go to talk to the Guard," Carlos said.

"Don't they have a base? I heard they took over the Ingles shopping center. What are they doing at the gas station?" Duke asked.

"They set up the gas station as their 'central office.' They said it was for convenience, but I think it's to keep people from nosing around the compound."

"Can't have the proletariat knowing all their secrets, now can they?" Duke said.

But Jane and Duke were stonewalled at the central office, too. The stalwart Guard refused to release any information. Jane was beside herself. She paced the parking lot between the derelict gas pumps, racking her brain for a way to help Willa.

"This is ridiculous! How can they not tell us anything? I mean, even Before, you could get one of those police report newspapers at any gas station." It was hard to tell if she was talking to Duke or herself.

"There's nothing we can do, Jane," Duke said. "I'll ask around, see if I can find anything out, but it looks like we're just gonna have to wait."

Chapter Eighteen

After two days of nervous pacing, Jane and Duke left their cabin to go to the stables. She was driving herself crazy worrying about Willa; she needed a distraction. Duke went back to rambling on about football. Jane tried her best to listen to him, but she was distracted as soon as they stepped into the road.

The intersection had transformed overnight. Jane and Duke stared slack-jawed at the new addition. A massive wooden platform had been erected. It took up most of the open space in the middle of the intersection. They approached it with cautious curiosity. Several people were doing the same thing. A handful of citizens stood on the porch of the coffee shop watching the crowd.

"What in the hell is this?" Jane breathed.

"A very, very bad sign," Duke replied.

The platform was chest high. A short set of steps led up to it. In the center of the platform, there were several T-bars made of logs mounted in a square. Each of the bars had ropes tied around the posts. The pungent scent of raw, cut pine hung in the air.

Jane looked up at Duke. "You don't think they're going to tie people to those things?"

"That's exactly what I think."

"That's completely medieval! It's—" She struggled to find the words.

"Barbaric?" Duke supplied.

"Yes. Why would they do that?"

"Same reason medieval people did it. Public humiliation."

Jane shook her head. "Let's get out of here."

It had been a while since Duke had ridden and he missed Max. Max trotted up to Duke as soon as he saw him. Duke rubbed his nose while Max sniffed his pockets looking for treats. Jane couldn't get over just how impressively large Max was. He stomped his dinner-plate-sized hooves.

The place was buzzing with gossip, mostly about Willa's behavior. A pair of women in clean, stylish riding gear and helmets whispered to each other while a stable-hand ran back and forth preparing a pair of horses for them to ride. They kept stealing glances at Jane and Duke. A stable-hand led Max and Mahz out to them. They went into the tack room and got their saddles. When they came back out, the women were mounted on their horses. They glanced back at Jane, then looked at each other and giggled. Jane flushed red, but Duke took it in stride.

"Don't worry about them. I bet they're part of the Chosen Ones."

"Chosen Ones?"

"Well, that's what they are, right? Hand-picked to populate their ideal sheep herd."

Before Jane could respond, Jennifer walked up with a couple of her friends. They all wore the same black helmets and held riding crops.

"That was some trick you pulled the other night."

Jane stared at her in disbelief. "What? The rodeo? You're still hung up on that? For Pete's sake, Jennifer, get over yourself."

Jennifer ignored her and went on with her attempt to humiliate Jane. "Too bad it meant you were disqualified."

"So? My time was still better than yours. Besides, what difference does it make? You didn't make the top three anyway."

The smug smile slid from her face. She leaned in and whispered, "I hope that bitch sister of yours gets what she deserves. That was my best bridle."

Jane frowned. "How do you know what was taken? The guard wouldn't release that information. Unless..." Jane's eyes widened with sudden realization. "You did this. You lied."

The smug grin was back. "And if I did, so what? There's nothing you can do about it. Who are they going to believe? An upstanding citizen, or questionable local?"

Jane snapped. She launched herself at Jennifer and tackled her. She lost track of how many blows she had managed to land. Duke looked around and saw three Guards running toward them. He wrapped his arm around Jane's waist and lifted her straight up. Jane fought against Duke as he pulled her off Jennifer. She kicked hard and managed to make contact with Jennifer's nose. Blood poured out of it, staining her shirt. She wailed in pain as her friends pulled her to her feet. The Guards aimed their guns at Duke, who had pinned Jane's back to his chest, his arms trapping hers to her sides. Her wild curls stood on end as she struggled.

"Put me down, dammit!" She hadn't noticed the Guards.

"Put her down now." It was Sergeant Smith. He strode up to Duke. "I said put her down."

Duke snarled at him but put Jane back down. As soon as her feet touched the ground, the Guards rushed forward. They shoved her to the ground with much more force than was necessary. Her face smacked the ground hard and she coughed as the stirred dust swirled around her. Someone jerked her arms back and cuffed her.

"We've had problems out of your brother and sister, but I honestly didn't expect the same behavior from you. Though, in hindsight, I should have. You do come from the same, low-grade stock." Sergeant Smith strolled up, his hands behind his back.

"Listen here, asshole—" Duke was outraged at the insult.

Sergeant Smith rounded on him. "Don't start shit with me, boy." He turned back to the Guards. "Take her to the square. She will make the perfect example for our new installation."

The Guards took her back to the intersection. Jane was led up the steps. The Guards jerked her arms back behind her, over the T-bar. Her wrists were tied to the post with the rope.

"You will stand here for the next forty-eight hours," Sergeant Smith said. He turned to the crowd that had followed them. "Let this woman be a lesson to you all. Violence will not be tolerated in this community."

He turned and climbed back down the steps without a backward glance. Duke was standing at the foot of the steps, his arms folded across his chest, a rare look of anger and hatred on his face. Smith looked up at him.

"You are not to look at her, talk to her, talk about her, until her time is served, or you will suffer the same punishment." He stormed off.

"What about food? You gonna feed her?"

"The human body can go weeks without food. She'll be fine for two days."

Chapter Nineteen

Willa was released from the labor camp the next day. Her face was sunburned and her hands were blistered. She was sweaty, dirty, and her matted, greasy hair was pulled up in a ponytail. Duke caught her before she made it all the way into town.

"What'd they have you do?" he asked.

"Digging graves. I'm exhausted and I haven't bathed in three days. I need to go home, get a bath, and take a sixteen hour nap. Where's Jane?"

Duke made a face, uncertain how to tell her what happened. "Before you freak out, listen—"

"Where is Jane?" she demanded. Something bad had happened. She knew it.

Duke conceded. "Okay, but don't freak out. And whatever you do, don't say anything to her."

A look of fear and confusion fell over Willa. She strode into town, Duke half a step behind. When she reached the square, she gasped and began to run towards the platform.

"Jane!" she screamed.

Duke caught her around the middle and stopped her. "You can't talk to her or they'll put you up there too. Not a good thing to do the first five minutes after getting out of the labor camp."

He waited until he was sure she wouldn't struggle before letting her go.

"What the hell happened while I was gone?"

Duke explained Jennifer's antagonizing and Jane's reaction.

"About damned time somebody put that bitch in her place." Willa just happened to see Jennifer across the square. Both of her eyes were black and purple and she sported a golf ball sized knot on her forehead.

There were several people tied to posts on either side of Jane. It did not escape anyone's notice that all of them were locals.

"What are the rest of them up there for?"

"For anything the Guard wants. Slander. Theft. Murder."

"Murder?" Willa's eyes went wide.

"No, not really. The old man died in his sleep. Didn't stop the Guard from charging his son for killing him."

"Why would they do that?"

Duke shrugged. "He's been mouthing off, probably. Saying something that contradicts them. They'll probably hang him later."

Duke stopped talking. His attention was captured by the appearance of Sergeant Smith on the platform, oddly enough, with Jennifer by his side. The two people tied on either side of Jane were moved to other posts farther away. Jane was left on her own, the center of attention for the growing crowd.

Willa looked at Duke in confusion.

"I dunno," he replied. "Let's go hide in the crowd."

They immersed themselves in the dense crowd. Everyone was so absorbed by the spectacle, no one noticed as they moved closer to the platform right in front of Jane.

Willa caught Jane's eye. *You okay?*

Jane's chin trembled, imperceptible to anyone but Willa. She was terrified. But she maintained a blank composure. She held Willa's gaze.

I'm scared.

Willa pursed her lips and nodded. *I know. Just hold on.*

Sergeant Smith approached Jane and sneered.

"There are still many of you that think that you can subvert the law. That you can disregard our authority and disrespect the more esteemed members of our community," he said to the crowd. "I have been thinking long and hard how to make you people understand that this is no longer a democracy. This town is under martial law and under my command. And for some reason, you seem to rally around this woman."

He gestured at Jane. Jane looked at Willa in bewilderment. *What the hell is he talking about?*

Willa returned an amused grin. *I guess you're more popular than you thought.*

"Well, ladies and gentlemen, today you are going to learn what happens to those who speak out against us. From here on out, I am implementing an 'eye for an eye' punishment regime. And we are going to start with our friend Jane Campbell, who thought she could beat up our beloved Jennifer Smith. Jennifer, the floor is yours."

He stepped aside and Jennifer took his place in front of Jane. Jane took one last glance at Willa before her attention was completely taken by the blonde in front of her. She swallowed hard, forcing the bubbling anxiety back down. She stood up as straight as she could.

"Do you have anything to say for yourself?" Jennifer asked.

"You know this won't save your reputation, right?"

The crowd was silent. They weren't raising their voices but their words rang loud and clear across the square. Jennifer back handed her. A collective gasp from the crowd. Nuke barked and tried to run to the platform, but Duke held him back.

"This isn't about making an example of me. This is about that stupid rodeo."

Jennifer smacked her again. She grabbed a lock of Jane's hair and twisted it, yanking on it. Jane winced.

"This is about your insolence and disrespect," Jennifer hissed.

"No, this is about me humiliating you in front of God and everybody."

Jennifer screeched and yanked the twist of hair out of Jane's scalp. Jane let out an involuntary yelp, but she wasn't about to back down.

"This is about me beating you at your own game at the rodeo."

Jennifer planted a fist in Jane's jaw. Another collective gasp from the crowd. Willa was beside herself with rage. Duke kept a hand on her shoulder, reminding her where she was.

Jane flexed her jaw. "This is about me beating your ass fair and square. The only way you have any chance of beating me is when I've got my hands tied."

Whispers and snickers swept across the crowd like dry leaves in a stiff breeze. Jennifer screamed again and sank a fist in Jane's stomach, knocking the wind out of her. Jane gasped and coughed. Jennifer continued to pull and twist Jane's hair. It didn't help matters that Jane was tender-headed. It was the only thing that elicited tears. After a while, Jennifer's fingers began to catch on the tangles and knots she had created.

Jennifer rained blow after blow on Jane, in her face, her chest. Jane felt her ribs crack under Jennifer's fists. Another blow to the jaw. Jane's lip split. Blood filled her numb mouth and dribbled down her chin. Eventually, she couldn't hold herself up anymore. She sank as far as her arms would let her. Jennifer bent down and whispered in her ear.

"Try anything again, *anything*, and I swear to God I'll kill you myself."

Jane's body convulsed with uncontrollable shivers. She only wore what she had been wearing when she was arrested: a t-shirt, sweatshirt, and jeans. Her leather boots kept her toes warm but her fingers were numb from the cold and lack of circulation. Her ears were so cold they hurt.

The sun had set over an hour ago. There was a new moon that night, leaving Jane in pitch black darkness. The only sounds were of the coughs and shivering breaths of the prisoners around her. In just the few hours between her arrest and the fall of night, four other locals were arrested on innocuous charges. She could hear them whispering to each other but no one dared speak to her. They blamed Jane for their predicament. Her arrest had set the Guard off on a spree. They were on a roll and didn't stop until lights out.

There were footsteps coming up the small set of steps and across the platform toward her.

"Please," Jane begged, her shuddering voice barely more than a sigh, "please just let me rest."

"Ssshh." It was Willa.

"What the hell are you doing here? You're gonna get caught."

"Not if you shut your damn mouth."

A soft bird whistle cut through the darkness. Duke was there, on the ground near the platform. He didn't come up, keeping watch below instead. Rather, soft tapping footsteps climbed the steps and crossed the platform. Nukem's soft, warm body sat at her feet and leaned against her legs.

A scarf appeared in the darkness and wrapped around Jane's frozen hands. A knit cap was pulled down over her ears. A blanket wrapped around her shoulders. All of these things were warm with Willa's body heat. Jane could smell her sister's unique scent on the blanket, a blend of horse hair, soap, and cigarettes. The tension in Jane's muscles relaxed all at once, making her knees weak. But she couldn't relax her knees without putting increased strain on the ropes around her wrists. Her hands were already numb and tingling. It took tremendous effort to hold herself up. A stiff plastic straw poked her in the face.

"Ow!"

"Sorry. Trying to find your mouth," Willa giggled. Fingers probed Jane's face. She winced. "Sorry." Willa found Jane's mouth and gave her the straw. Jane took a tentative sip of warm chicken broth. Each and every movement sent shooting pains through her chest from her cracked ribs. Jane took small, slow sips of the warm broth. When she finished, Willa walked around the other side of Jane's post and stood back to back with her sister. Jane laid her head back on Willa's shoulder. She closed her eyes, eternally grateful for the support, physically and emotionally.

"You've gotta get out of here, Willa."

"I will. Just shut up and rest a minute."

Jane fell silent. She allowed a few tears to escape and roll down her bruised and swollen face.

"I shouldn't have hit her," Jane whispered.

"Hell yes, you should have. I'm so damned proud of you. Standing up to her. Bitch got what she had coming."

Jane shook her head against Willa's shoulder. "Yes, but I could've found another way to give it to her. I'm always the one saying violence isn't the answer."

"Yeah," Willa agreed, "but it just goes to show what kind of person she is, if she can goad you of all people into a fist fight. God I wish I had been there to see it."

She must have fallen asleep because the next thing she knew, she was being shaken awake. Willa was moving to leave. She took back the scarf, hat, and blanket. The cold crashed through Jane like a wave and she began to shiver again.

"They're letting you go tomorrow. I'll be back in a little while." With that, Willa disappeared into the darkness. "C'mon, Nuke."

Nukem refused to leave. He sat between Jane's legs, giving her what soft warmth he could.

Sergeant Smith finally allowed Jane to be cut down from her post. Her legs were so weak she couldn't stand. Her arms were stiff and throbbed from the awkward position and lack of circulation they had endured for the last two days. Duke put his arms under her legs and around her back. He lifted her as gently as he could, but she cried out at the slightest touch. Duke carried her back to the cabin. The crowd that had gathered tried to follow them back. Carlos was there too, helping them cut a path through the crowd. Willa yelled herself hoarse at them.

"This is all a show to you. You don't give a damn about her. Or any of us for that matter."

The locals looked down in shame, the Chosen Ones just sneered.

"I'm just gonna lay you on my bed," Duke said to Jane. "It's easier than carrying you to the loft."

"You haven't spent a night at home all week, anyway. It's not like it's an inconvenience," Jane said.

Duke had tried to be inconspicuous about it, but all three of them were too aware of each other's presence for his absence to go unnoticed. Since the rodeo, Duke spent almost every night somewhere other than his bed in the cabin. Jane and Willa didn't say anything to him. Living in such close proximity to each other for so long, privacy was at a minimum. There was an unspoken agreement to respect what little privacy they had and not into each other's business.

"Yeah. Where have you been, anyway?" Willa looked at him with indignant suspicion. Now that Jane had brought it up, Willa felt the need to ask, especially with everything that had happened.

Duke laid Jane on the bed. "Teaching calculus to goats." He took his hat off, only to resettle it back on his head. "That's not important right now. We've got more pressing things to worry about right now."

They propped Jane up on a stack of pillows where she stared out the window, refusing to look anyone in the eye. Her face was swollen and purple. Red and purple welts wound around her wrists, cutting deep into her flesh. Jennifer had twisted her hair into painful tangles and knots. Willa knew from a long childhood of dealing with Jane's unruly hair that it would be a nightmare to get it back to normal.

"Jane is usually the one stitching us up," Willa told Carlos. "It's not usual that she's the one in need of stitching. I'm going to go get a nurse from the medical center."

"Won't do any good," Carlos said. "They won't treat injuries resulting from punishment. Lucky for you, I'm a registered nurse. Used to be, anyway."

"You? A nurse?" Willa was surprised. "I pegged you for more of the starving artist type."

"Why do you think I got into nursing? Starving artist doesn't pay the bills. Or, didn't, rather."

Willa left to fetch Maria while Carlos looked Jane over. They returned with warm water, antiseptic, and bandages. Willa did as she always did: helping as she could, handing Carlos supplies as he needed them, and generally trying to stay out of the way.

He cut away her shirt so she wouldn't have to pull it over her head. Her chest and stomach were just as bruised as everything else. None of them had ever been so excessively injured, especially at the hands of another person. It was a feeling none of them could fathom. Willa felt each wound as if they were her own. Jane was a good person. Better than she was. Jane didn't deserve this. Jane hadn't spoken a word. She winced and cried out while Carlos tended to her wounds but still did not speak.

Duke stood outside the room, out of privacy, but he could still hear her cries. He'd never felt this helpless before. He wanted to help, but he didn't know what to do. Stressful ordeals always affected Jane more than him or Willa. He knew the torment she was bottling up inside and it pained him that he was powerless to stop it.

"It hurts to breathe," Jane whispered. Tears streamed down her face.

"It looks like a couple of your ribs are cracked. This is going to hurt like hell but I need to tape your ribs. Can you sit up for me?"

Gingerly, he pulled her into a sitting position. Jane wailed.

"There we go." Carlos had slipped into his reassuring nurse voice. "Willa help her sit up while I tape her ribs."

Willa took Jane's hands and held her up while Carlos worked.

She squeezed her sister's hands gently and gave her a weak smile.

After Carlos finished, he pulled Duke aside. "I've got an idea. C'mon."

Duke whistled at Nuke to follow, but the dog ignored him. Nuke curled up next to Jane and licked her hand. Duke just nodded. Nuke knew she needed him more than Duke did. Duke and Carlos left, leaving Willa and Maria to watch over Jane. Willa went back into the living room, giving Jane a chance for some much-needed rest, but it never came. They sat there, listening to Jane cry.

"How is she?" Maria asked. She'd been in the kitchen, staying out of the way.

"She's in a lot of pain. And hungry, I'm sure. Can you find her something to eat? Something easy to chew."

"Of course." She got up and left.

Willa peeked in on Jane. She was on her side, her back to the door. She clutched a pillow as her chest rose and fell in painful breaths. Willa couldn't stand it and walked outside. She paced back and forth across the little screened in porch. She looked up at the sound of footsteps crunching on the gravel. It was Duke and Carlos carrying what looked like a plastic sink and a chair. Maria was just behind them with a large plastic pitcher.

"We stole this from the salon down the road," Carlos said. It was a beautician's chair, a hair washing sink, and several bottles of conditioner. "Momma Dee supplied the conditioner. Many of my family have curly hair like hers. I saw what that girl did to her hair. I understand her pain. You'll have to make do with buckets of water, but I thought this would help."

Willa ran to him and hugged him. "Thank you."

They set the chair and sink up in the small kitchenette. Carefully, Jane settled into the chair. Maria heated buckets of water while Willa worked through the tangled mess. There were several places where Jennifer had pulled out great chunks of hair altogether. Jane whimpered and cried through most of it. Willa's heart ached for her sister.

After an hour of painstaking detangling, Jane's hair finally fell limp and wet against her neck. Willa towel dried it as best she could, but did what she could not to tug on it. They helped her drink some of the broth that Maria had brought back from Momma Dee. Eventually, Jane fell asleep. Willa walked back into the living room. Duke was asleep on the couch. Willa shook him awake.

"I'm gonna stay down here in case she needs me," Willa said. "You can go sleep upstairs for now."

Duke sat up and rubbed his eyes. "Nah. I gotta go."

"Now? It's ten o'clock at night! What the hell do you have to do this late?"

"I've got a, uh, thing that I, uh…yeah. Don't worry about it. I'll be back in the morning." Duke picked up his hat and adjusted it on his head.

"Oh yeah. That's not suspicious at all." Willa rolled her eyes.

He slipped his boots on and walked out the door.

Two days later, Willa heard Jane moving around downstairs. She got up, assuming Jane needed help with something. She found Jane on the couch, fully dressed, struggling to reach down to tie her shoes.

"What are you doing?"

"I'm going into town."

"Why?"

"We need eggs."

Willa gave her a disapproving look. "We do not need eggs and you do not need to go into town. You need to rest."

"I'm fine."

"You just got the holy hell beaten out of you. You haven't slept in three days. You were up all night last night. I heard you crying."

"Yes, I was. At night, I can get all my crying and anxiety and whatever out. But it's daylight now."

"What are you trying to prove? This isn't like you."

Jane stopped struggling with her shoes and looked up at Willa. "This is what she wants. She wants me beaten and defeated. She wants me to cower and cry, and with that she has succeeded."

"Then why go out there and face it all over again?"

"She has torn me down to the studs but she doesn't need to know that. My face may still be swollen and bruised, but my hair is back to normal, the stiffness in my arms and legs is mostly gone. I can stand and walk on my own. The best thing I can do is go out there, my shoulders back, and my middle finger in the air."

Never in her life had Willa felt more proud of Jane than she did in that moment. "At least let me do your makeup."

"No. I'm not going to cover it up. I want them to see what their cowardly actions have done and that they don't affect me."

"But they do affect you. You can't even put on your shoes."

Jane looked at Willa, then went back to putting on her shoes. "Like I said, they don't need to know that."

Chapter Twenty

By the middle of December, Jane's ribs had healed considerably, but they still ached if she moved too much. She may have been on the mend, but life in Cashiers Village had deteriorated quickly. Every other day, new laws were enacted, bringing the villagers under the iron fist of what Smith called "the beginning of a better, brighter future."

Strict curfews were put into place. Not that many people were out after dark anyway. Winter came roaring in with blistering winds that forced people inside. With the short winter days and bitter cold, many people were forced to quit work early, leaving them with less money and less food. More and more people signed up for rations, but the rations had been reduced to the point that it didn't help much anyway. The poorest villagers were beginning to starve.

Christmas was just a week away, but the mood in town could not have been less merry. Additional T-posts were added around the edge of the platform to accommodate the increased number of people arrested for stealing food. Willa and Carlos had been sending their teams in search of toys and gifts for the children at the Home, stockpiling them in a desperate attempt to distract them from their growling bellies.

Willa followed Jane into town, worried that she might fall or, worse, have a panic attack. Jane took slow, carefully measured steps. Jane's bruised face was beginning to fade from dark shades of purple to a mottled swirl of blue and yellow. A few of them waved. Jane smiled and waved back. Jennifer stood on the porch of the old coffee shop, glaring at them. Jane smiled and waved at her too. Willa flipped her off. People gawked at them and whispered to each other as they crossed the street to Momma Dee's.

"If I do that, you're all going to get sick, every one of you." Momma Dee had her arms crossed.

"And I'm telling you now, if that happens, you'll be held responsible. You will cater this dinner. You will serve what you are told to serve, and you will keep your damned mouth shut. Understood?" Sergeant Smith growled.

Momma Dee shook her head. "Fine. I'll do your damned dinner, but I'm going to make sure everybody knows that it was you who insisted on this. I tried to tell you. I tried to talk you out of it. If it's anybody's fault, it'll be yours."

"We'll see about that." He turned to storm off, but he caught sight of Willa and Jane. He turned back to Momma Dee. "Make sure these two are there."

Jane stared at him as he walked away. She turned to Momma Dee. "What was that all about?"

"Apparently there's going to be some big Christmas dinner for all the high ranking Guards and their families. I have to cater it."

"What's going to make people sick?"

"He wants seafood, of all things."

Jane was surprised. "Seafood? How? You'll have to go all the way to the coast for that. Even Before, that was a six hour drive, but now..."

"That's a three day trip, minimum, if you factor in time to round up that much seafood and work out a deal. Then to transport it all the way back up here? We don't have refrigeration. It'll spoil. You're damn right, people will get sick." Willa was indignant.

"When is the dinner?" Jane asked.

"Next Saturday."

"You're shitting me. That's Christmas Eve!"

Momma Dee sighed and rubbed her temples. "I wish I was.

Willa, you work with the Searchers. Is there any way you can make this trip?"

Momma Dee looked weary. Willa knew it wasn't her fault.

"Yeah. I'll get it done. I'll go talk to the guys. The sooner we leave the better. And what did he mean, make sure we're there? To serve?"

Momma Dee nodded. "Yeah. I guess so."

"That bastard. He's got it in for us." Willa stood and looked down at Jane. "Will you be okay on your own?"

"Yeah. Go ahead. I'll be fine."

Willa left and headed to the fire station. She stormed down the road with murder in her eyes. People cut a wide berth to stay out of her path. Just as she was about to open the door, she happened to see Laura standing by the front door of the Home, smoking a cigarette, baby Grace playing on the sidewalk beside her. Willa walked over to her. As she got closer, she could see just how utterly exhausted she was. Laura leaned against the brick wall, her eyes closed.

"Don't fall asleep," Willa said, getting her attention.

Laura looked up at Willa with bloodshot eyes. "Oh. Hey."

"Dude, are you okay?" Willa was concerned about how tired Laura looked.

"I'm fine. I just need a nap."

"You look like the dead. When was the last time you slept?"

"I had a couple hours about..." She looked at her watch. "About forty hours ago."

"Jeez, Laura. Why don't you take a break?"

Laura shook her head and took a drag of her cigarette.

"I can't. A lot of the kids are getting sick. It's taking our attention from the other kids. Some of the guys from the station have been helping when they can but it's turned into a round the clock thing."

"What's wrong with them?"

"It's some kind of flu. But it's so much worse than what we're used to dealing with. We had a flu outbreak last year, but it was nothing compared to this. It's spreading like wildfire. We've got the sick kids separated but all it takes is one of them to so much as sneeze on us and we've passed it to the other kids. It's even starting to spread through the older folks that live here. Two of them are already sick."

"What about medicine? Doesn't the Guard have something they can give them?"

"Not really. They gave us some but it wasn't enough for everybody, and they said it was all they had. We're down to nothing. I don't know what to do." Her voice cracked. Poor Laura was at her wit's end.

Willa put her hands on Laura's shoulders. "Look at me Laura." Laura looked up, the fear in her eyes pleaded for an answer. "I'm going to go get Jane. She's going to help you so you can get some sleep. I have to make a long trip with the searchers. It's a long story but we'll be gone for several days. Tell me what medicine you need and we'll look for it while we're gone."

Laura looked at Willa like she was a gift from God. She wrapped her arms around Willa's neck and began to weep.

"Thank you. Thank you so much."

Willa returned the hug. She picked up Grace.

"How about I babysit while I go find Jane."

"Are you sure?"

"Absolutely. Sit. Rest for a little bit."

Laura didn't bother finding a chair. She sank to the ground where she stood and fished for another cigarette. With Grace tucked into the crook of her arm, Willa turned back to go find Jane again. The anger in Willa's heart melted when she looked at Grace's chubby smile. Willa grinned and tickled her belly. Grace's bright blue eyes sparkled as she giggled. She stuffed her little fist in her mouth, then wiped her slobbery hand on Willa's cheek.

Tears welled up behind Willa's eyes. Emma's eyes may have been brown rather than Grace's bright blue, and her hair might have been a darker shade of brown, but Grace's shrill squeals and chubby fingers reminded Willa so much of her Emma. She remembered Emma's sweet smile, her wild crown of dark curls that looked so much like her aunt.

Willa tickled Grace again. Willa smiled wider than she had in months and laughed. Grace doubled over and laid her head on Willa's shoulder. She squirmed and climbed around in Willa's arms, trying to escape the tickles. She was so happy and so blissfully unaware of the dangerous world she lived in. Willa knew in her heart that it didn't matter that this little girl wasn't her Emma. It didn't matter. She would do whatever it took to protect her.

Chapter Twenty-One

"Does everyone understand the plan?" Willa looked around at the group of people around her. A collective murmur of agreement.

Willa had left Grace in Jane's care while she rounded up her team of searchers. She had told Jane about Laura and the kids at the Home. Jane didn't hesitate. She had strapped Grace on her own back with the carrier. Jane couldn't fathom what Willa felt but she knew that Willa would rather die herself than to watch those kids suffer like her daughter did.

"Good. Go pack a bag. We leave in an hour." She turned to Duke, who walked up with Nuke just as Willa dismissed them. "Where the hell have you been? We haven't seen you in two days."

"I keep telling you. Goats. Calculus." He pulled off his hat, scratched his head, and put it back on again. "Anyway, the forge is down. Somebody dropped a handful of shotgun shells in the forge and blew the thing all to hell."

"Somebody, huh? And no one knows who."

"Nope. No clue." Duke adjusted his hat.

Willa didn't believe him for a minute. "So what are you doing here?"

"Jane said you were here. I heard about this little mission and thought I'd lend a hand," Duke said.

"It's gonna be a good trip." Carlos was excited. "It's been a long time since we've found anything good."

"The most important thing is the medicine. We've got to find something for those kids," Willa said.

They drove through the night made it to the coast the following morning. It took all day to find what they were looking for.

They finally found a little fish market on a long pier late in the afternoon. At the far end of the pier, a dozen men were packing up at least two dozen poles and hauling tubs of fish back to the pier house. Waves crashed around the struts at the end of the pier as the tide went out. Many of the boards that made up the pier had been recently replaced. They were smoother and much lighter in color and stood out against the darker boards that were well worn from the salt water. The air was thick with the pungent odor of fish.

A man came out of the little fishing hut. He had a thick gray beard and black rubber boots that came to his knees. He looked like he'd never smiled in his life, nor had any intention to.

"What do you want?" he growled without even a hello.

Willa took the hint and skipped the formalities. "We want to buy some seafood. Enough for at least fifty people. Shrimp, fish, anything to cater a party."

His eyebrows drew together. "The whole damn country is gone to pot and you're throwing a party?"

"Believe me, it's not mine. I think the whole thing is bullshit. I'm just the runner."

He regarded her for a moment. "I got some tuna fillets, plenty of oysters and mussels, but I can't spare much shrimp."

"Just give me what you can. I'll take it. I'm not in much of a position to be picky."

The man nodded and whistled to some of his fishermen. Willa waved at her crew and they started unloading the coolers. It took over an hour to load up all the seafood and make a deal. The fishermen didn't ask many questions, but they did cast curious and confused glances at their lack of refrigeration. Even their coolers were warm to the touch.

With the foreman's permission, the crew made a little camp

fire on the beach by the pier and took the opportunity to relax a little bit. Some of the fishermen came down with beers and they sat around the fire drinking and swapping stories. Willa didn't feel much like drinking. She sat a little way away, her arms around her knees, watching the waves crash against the sand. She pulled her coat tighter around herself as a cold ocean breeze tugged at her hair. The full moon reflected on the water; the waves scattered the bright light across its surface like diamonds tumbling across a table.

She heard footsteps coming toward her, but she didn't look up. Duke and Carlos sat down on either side of her. Carlos handed her a dark brown bottle. She took it but didn't drink it.

"It's not like you to stew quietly." Duke read the room and knew it wasn't the time for one of his smartass comments. "I figured you'd be pacing around til dawn."

Willa spun the bottle around and around in her hands and continued to stare at the horizon. "It's just occurred to me just how vastly alone we are."

"Well, I wouldn't call it vast. I mean the crew is out of ear shot, but they can still see us," Carlos said.

"No, I mean all of us. The country. The survivors." She pointed at the horizon. "Directly in front of us is the coast of Africa, and beyond that all of Europe and Asia. Right across this ocean are millions of people carrying on with their lives, with the Internet and Starbucks and the stock market and all of the shit that makes life modern. And yet, here we are, with a truck full of warm coolers full of spoiling fish, driving a truck that runs on propane, going back to a town that isn't much better off than it was a hundred years ago. And there's nothing we can do about it. There's nothing anyone can do about it."

"It won't last," Duke said. "It's like I said before, you can't take that kind of control and expect to hold on to it for very long. We'll get help eventually."

She looked at Duke. "But even when we do, it won't be enough to rebuild everything. Our country is going to be like this for a very long time. No matter how much help we get, if we get any at all, we will still be so vastly alone. And there's nothing we can do about it."

⁂

The following day, they struck out for home. It took twice as long to get back as it did to go down. There wasn't room in the vehicles to carry extra tanks so they had to stop several times to find propane. Each time they stopped, Willa sent a handful of searchers out to look for medicine. To her dismay, they found little. She wanted to make a thorough search, looking through doctor and patient files to find their addresses and search their homes. But they were running out of time, and she knew what consequences would await her if she didn't return in time, or if she allowed the food to spoil any more than it would already.

"So, uh, what's the deal with Willa?" Carlos asked.

They were just outside of Charlotte, picking their way through the stalled cars on the interstate. Nuke was in the back, sticking his head out in the wind. They were in the last truck in their little convoy, following the rest of the crew back to the Village. Most of the crew was crammed into the Expedition at the head of the convoy. The Durango in the middle carried the coolers full of seafood. Duke and Carlos were in the old Ford at the end of the line. It was loaded down with supplies they had scavenged, and the cab was small, so they were spared from having to share their limited space with anyone else.

"What do you mean?" Duke was driving and stole a glance at Carlos.

"Well, she doesn't seem interested in dating anybody. Is she, uh, holding out for someone, or..."

"Oh, I get it. Sorry, man. I don't think she's interested in being interested in anyone right now. Jane either. Too much going on right now, ya know?"

"Oh, okay. Yeah. I get it." Carlos looked disappointed. He was quiet for a moment, as if steeling himself. "What about you?"

"What about me?" Duke was genuinely confused for a moment, until, "Oh. OH!" Duke blushed. "Look man. I'm flattered, honestly, but I'm, uh, not cross-platform compatible."

Carlos flushed crimson. "Oh. Jeez. I'm sorry, amigo. I didn't mean to make you uncomfortable."

Duke laughed and clapped him on the shoulder. "Nah man. I understand. It's not like I've got a sticker on my forehead that says "Rated E for Everyone."

"So, you're not weirded out?"

"Of course not. We're still bros." Duke held up his fist.

Carlos relaxed and fist bumped him.

"Dude! Look!" Duke pointed at a billboard for a fireworks superstore. "What do you say we stock up?"

Duke flashed his lights at Willa in the Durango. She stopped and Duke told her what they wanted to do.

"Fine." She shrugged. Her mind was clearly elsewhere. "You know how to get back. Just don't take too long."

A tearful Laura wrapped her arms around Willa's neck. "Thank you. Thank you so much."

Willa hugged her back. "I'm so sorry, Laura. It's all we could find. We didn't have time to look for more."

They had only found enough to treat five of the children, but dozens had become ill in the few days that she had been gone.

"Please don't give up. I'll keep looking. I swear."

The front door opened. They turned to see Nora in the doorway.

"It's okay, sweetie." Laura swept away her tears and put on a smile. "Mommy's okay. Come here."

Nora came out and wrapped her arms around Laura's waist. Laura stooped and brushed Nora's hair out of her face. As soon as her hands touched Nora's skin, her smile slipped away. Nora was burning with fever.

"I don't feel good, Mommy," Nora whispered. She leaned forward and buried her face in her mother's neck. Laura wrapped her arms around Nora and looked up at Willa. Laura's eyes begged Willa for a miracle.

Chapter Twenty-Two

Willa tugged at the collar of her uniform. Laura had dug out a set of uniforms she and Jane had worn when they worked as waitresses at the Country Club. For Jane, the uniform felt familiar and oddly comforting. Willa, who had never worked anywhere that required a uniform, felt like she was being strangled by the high collar of the white button down shirt and black neck tie.

They were standing in the kitchen of the Wade Hampton Country Club with a dozen other waitstaff, waiting for their cue to enter the dining room, each with their own tray of glasses of champagne. Momma Dee was in her element, the queen of the kitchen, overseeing all, and all looking to her for direction.

"This is ridiculous," Willa snapped. "I've got better shit to do than walk around and cater to these assholes."

Willa was anxious to get back to the station. She had sent her search team West toward Chattanooga. She didn't expect them back until the following evening, but she was desperate to find the medication and had begun to feel anxious anytime she was away from the station and the Home.

The cue came for the waitstaff to enter the dining room and begin making their way through the crowd with the first round of drinks and shrimp cocktails. It was only 7:30. Dinner wouldn't be served until nine o'clock.

The atmosphere was almost magical. Frosted Christmas trees sparkled in every corner. Pine bough and streams of tinsel hung from every rafter and banister. The guests were dressed in their finest glittering gowns and sharpest tuxedos. The bulbs overhead sparkled in the ornate chandeliers and cast glimmering lights on the walls and ceiling. Gentle, lilting music from the string band in the corner mingled with the soft murmur of conversation and tinkling laughter. The extravagance made Jane feel ill.

Jane made her way around the left side of the room while Willa went around the right. Jane and Willa didn't work side by side. Rather, they took opposite sides of the room, always maintaining a wide view and always watching each other. While Willa struggled to remain civil with the guests she was serving, Jane was in her element. After ten years in retail and food service, Jane knew exactly how to stroke the egos of those with more money than sense. Jane joked, smiled, and laughed her way around the room, knowing that she would eventually cross paths with Willa in the middle.

With one glass left on her tray, Jane turned to the other side of the room, ready to mingle with the next group of wealthy residents. She pulled up short. She was face to face with Jennifer. She was standing by a long buffet table; her thin blonde hair had been painstakingly and elaborately curled and piled up high on her head. Her midnight blue gown did nothing to flatter her thin figure. Rather, it hung straight down from her shoulders like a sheer curtain around a dowel rod.

A cruel smile crept across her face and Jane knew it was she that had requested that Jane and Willa be there to serve. Jane felt the blood rush to her face. The swelling around her eyes had gone down considerably, but the bruises had proved difficult to conceal under makeup. Jane's heart began to hammer out an uneven beat. Her palms were clammy and damp, and her hands began to shake. She could see Willa over Jennifer's shoulder but she ignored her. Instead, she took a deep breath to steady herself, put on her best, fake public service smile and approached Jennifer as if she had never met her before.

"How are you tonight?" Jane offered a kind smile that wasn't quite as fake as the one she'd used with the other guests. She discreetly wiped the sweat from her palm before handing Jennifer the last glass of champagne from her tray.

"I'm well, thank you." Jennifer's smile, while pretending to be kind, was cruel and amused. "I see you're back up on your feet. How fortunate."

"Yes, I am fortunate to have people that care about me."

Jennifer scowled. "If you're implying that I don't have any friends—"

"Oh, I wasn't implying anything. I apologize if it came across that way." Jane was doing what she could to diffuse the tension between her and Jennifer, but Jennifer wasn't making it easy.

"I'll have you know I have many friends. In very high places. Friends who owe me favors."

"You don't have friends, Jennifer. You have a superiority complex, a well-connected father, and a couple of bimbos hanging onto your coattails," Willa said.

Laura had also made it to the table. She pretended to be adjusting a flower arrangement.

"You need to watch yourself." Jennifer rounded on Willa. "You need to learn your place in this world. The only reason you're here is to wear that uniform and carry that tray." Willa's face reddened. Her eyebrows drew together and her mouth tensed in a thin line. "I am not your fucking servant."

"Using profanity isn't ladylike."

"Well, neither is your mustache," Willa snapped.

Jane nearly dropped her tray. Laura hid behind the flower arrangement.

Jennifer gasped. "How dare you!"

Willa brushed past her. Jane followed as discreetly as she could, failing to stifle her laughter.

"Come back here and apologize."

Willa kept walking. Jennifer grabbed her arm and pulled her to a stop. They had stopped just in front of the kitchen doors.

"Did you not hear me? I said apologize."

"There's no need to repeat yourself. I ignored you just fine the first time. Oh, and by the way, next time you dye your hair, do your eyebrows too, so nobody knows that the carpet doesn't match the drapes."

Jennifer shrieked.

Willa pushed through the kitchen doors, grabbed a glass of champagne from the nearest tray, and downed it in a gulp. Jane clutched the steel table, doubled over in laughter. Her sore ribs weren't completely healed yet. They ached as she laughed but she couldn't stop.

At nine o'clock, the guests began to take their seats at the long dinner tables. The first course was a simple salad with fresh greens, carrots, onions, and cheese. As they sampled their salads, they placed their orders with the wait staff. A few ordered the prime rib, but the majority ordered the night's special: ahi tuna steaks.

Jane, Willa, and Laura worked their way around the tables, ladling lobster bisque into bowl after bowl. Willa worked in silence. Jane worked the crowd. Jane and Laura had walked countless laps around this dining room when they worked together. There was a certain finesse, they had learned, to working with and serving the wealthy and well to do, a delicate hand, a winning smile, and always make the conversation about them.

As the busboys cleared the soup bowls, Jane, Willa, and the others brought out the main course. The other waitstaff were oblivious to the situation, but Jane and Willa knew just how toxic the tuna was, not to mention the shrimp cocktails from earlier. They handled the plates and the guests like live bombs, talking softly and moving gently, as if loud noises or sudden movements might trigger the oncoming tsunami of food poisoning that was to come.

Dinner ended without incident. Willa breathed a sigh of relief, but Jane knew what was coming. And come it did, during after dinner drinks. At first, it was just one guest excusing herself to use the restroom. Then another. Then two more. Soon there was a line at the restroom.

Jennifer sauntered up to Jane, champagne glass in hand. She couldn't resist another opportunity to attack Jane.

"You seem to be healing well," Jane said amiably.

"Better than you, apparently. I'm surprised you didn't have to shave your head."

"Yes, I am very fortunate the parts of my hair that are missing are easily concealable." Jane's polite smile never wavered.

"What a pity. Even a bald head would look better than that rat's nest."

Jane dropped her professional tone and regarded Jennifer like an equal. "Look, I'm sorry for fighting you. I'm sorry I hurt you."

"It's about damned time you apologized. You should be sorry."

"Look, I know you don't like me. I don't like you either, but that doesn't excuse my behavior. We have to be the change we want to see in the world, and violence isn't the way to go about it."

"Oh, don't give me that 'holier than thou' bullshit. I—" Her haughty expression faded as her stomach gave an audible lurch. Her chin trembled. She set her glass down and turned to the restroom without another word.

The tone of conversation began to shift from relaxed and sated to upset and panicking. People were running from the dining room, desperate to find an unoccupied bathroom. Jane abandoned her professional persona and pushed through the crowd until she found Willa.

"We gotta go. Now."

They had just reached the swinging kitchen doors when they heard the first guest retch. A chain reaction soon followed, a cacophony of retching, coughing, screaming, and crying. There was no one left in the kitchen. All the staff were either in the dining room, dealing with the aftermath, or had fled. Jane and Willa joined those who had fled and made their way back to their cabin.

Chapter Twenty-Three

Two days passed. The village was a ghost town as the unfortunate guests recovered from the ordeal. The weather had taken another turn for the worse as a winter storm worked its way up the South East, forcing all of the other villagers to hunker down.

Willa had taken over the counter top with a map of Waynesville and a giant stack of files. She'd been working for months, mapping out the homes of medical personnel from every surrounding town. Jane spent those days in an unending state of panic, waiting for the inevitable. The front door crashed open, scaring Jane out of her wits.

"Jane!" Duke bellowed. "Willa! Get out here now!" He ran back outside without waiting for them.

It was rare for Duke to yell, much less for him to sound so panicked. Jane didn't hesitate. She hurtled down the stairs and met Willa in the living room. They exchanged a confused glance and followed him. Duke ran down the gravel path, through the parking lot and toward the park, Nuke at his heel. Willa and Jane struggled to keep up with his long stride.

Despite the weather, a large crowd was gathered on the Green, everyone facing the stage. Jane gasped when she saw why the crowd had gathered. Sergeant Smith stood at the dais. Beside him, standing on a stool, was Momma Dee. A noose, tied to the rafter above her, was wrapped around her neck. Her hands were bound behind her back. The sea of people parted around Duke and his sisters. They all turned and stared at them as they approached the front of the crowd.

Laura was on her knees in front of the crowd, sobbing. Willa ran and wrapped her arms around Laura. Jane's knees gave out. Duke caught her before she hit the ground.

"Many of you here today," Sergeant Smith began, "are not originally from this area. Some of you had friends and family here long before the world changed. Others came here after the world changed, and you were graciously welcomed into our community. Because now, more than ever, it is important to help our fellow man."

"They didn't seem so keen on helping their fellow man when we came to town," Duke whispered. Jane remembered their first day in Cashiers Village. The animosity at the processing center was tangible and hard to forget.

"But recently, a disturbing pattern has emerged. The local population, who have lived here all their lives, seem to become hostile toward those who have come from afar. They do not seem to care what sacrifices the new citizens have made for the betterment of this community.

"Why is it that the new citizens of Cashiers Village have more pride in this town than the rest of you that have lived here all your lives? These fine men and women have worked hard to make this town as prosperous as it is, and yet, they still do not receive the respect they deserve. As a matter of fact, some of you have even used violence against these upstanding citizens."

He stared around at the crowd. Jane looked around. A wide aisle cleaved the crowd, leaving the Chosen Ones on one side and the locals on the other. The Chosen Citizens glared at the crowd of locals.

"Last week, I held a Christmas dinner to honor these citizens and the contributions they have made. I made the grave mistake of hiring this woman," he motioned to Momma Dee without looking at her, "to cater the event. But unfortunately, she chose to use that opportunity to poison everyone there. I am here to tell you, all of you, that this blatant violence and disrespect will not be tolerated. I have been a generous and lenient governor, but no more.

"The justice system of the past is no longer applicable to our new world. Rehabilitation is not a viable option anymore. We do not have the time, energy, or resources to spare on keeping criminals locked up. It is a luxury we cannot afford. In this harsh new reality, if there is a threat, it must be eliminated."

The crowd of citizens roared with applause and malicious cheers.

"Mary Deborah Norris. You are hereby charged with thirty counts of attempted murder by poisoning." Sergeant Smith gripped the podium with both hands.

"I told you from the beginning those people would get sick. This is bullshit and you know it," Momma Dee interrupted him.

"You are guilty of the crimes you have been charged with. You are sentenced to hang by your neck until you are dead. Do you have anything you want to say?"

"My only regret is that you made my daughter sit here and watch this shit show. I'm just glad you didn't make my granddaughters watch it too. Go screw yourself, Smith."

Sergeant Smith didn't respond. He waved his hand, giving the signal to the Guard standing beside her. The Guard put his foot on the stool.

"I love you, Laura."

"I love you too, Momma," Laura sobbed.

The Guard kicked the stool out from under Momma Dee's feet. She dropped a few short feet until the rope snapped tight around her neck. She struggled for several minutes until finally falling still. Shock and disbelief fell over the crowd. Laura stopped crying. She just sat there staring at her mother's lifeless body.

Willa and Jane looked at Duke. Without needing to be told, he stepped forward and scooped Laura up into his arms. She didn't resist, she just laid her head on his shoulder, her eyes vacant and hollow. Duke carried Laura to their cabin, Willa and Jane a few steps behind. Maria fell into step beside Jane and put her hand in hers. Jane squeezed her hand.

The crowd was slow to disperse. Jane stopped to see what held their attention. The Guards cut down Momma Dee's body and loaded it in the back of a truck.

"Where are the girls?" Jane whispered.

"They're at the Home. Nora's worse. No need to upset her more. She doesn't need to know right now," Maria said.

The truck drove through town faster than they could walk through the park. By the time they got back to the intersection, the Guards were busy hanging Momma Dee from the traffic light with the other bodies. Duke placed a gentle hand on Laura's head, shielding her view.

Once in the cabin, Jane and Maria set about making coffee. Duke settled Laura on the couch before sitting in the recliner. Nuke leaped up on the couch and curled up next to Laura, putting his head in her lap. She rubbed his ears but didn't seem to realize he was there. Willa sat on the coffee table in front of Laura and held her hand.

"We will give her a nice funeral," Willa said. Rather than comforting her, Laura acted as if Willa's words caused her more pain.

"Actually," Maria's tone was full of sorrow, "there won't be a funeral."

The Campbells looked at her in shock. Laura just stared at the wall, tears streaming down her face.

Maria pressed a warm mug into Laura's hand. Laura didn't seem to notice.

"That's the law here now. They just posted it this morning. Anyone who is executed for a crime is not allowed to have a funeral. They say that because criminals were dishonorable people in life, they should not be honored in death. Their lives should not be celebrated," Maria explained.

"Smith did that on purpose. Just because of Momma Dee." There was a bitter edge rising in Jane's voice.

"They're afraid of creating martyrs out of people they've

eliminated as threats," Duke said sagely. The room fell silent, everyone caught up in their own tormented thoughts.

"This is BULLSHIT!" Jane slammed her hands down on the counter, making everybody jump. For the first time, Jane was properly outraged. "There is no absolutely no way I'm going to let Momma Dee rot from a streetlight."

For the first time since her arrival, Laura looked up. She stared at Jane. Her expression was still blank but deep in her eyes was a glimmer of hope.

"And what exactly do you propose we do?" Willa was skeptical.

"We'll hold a funeral anyway. We'll cut her down and take her to her grave ourselves."

"And what about the Guard? They'll try to stop us." Duke didn't sound skeptical. In fact, he was sitting forward in his seat, very much interested. It wasn't an excuse. It was a problem that needed a solution.

"We'll need people. A lot of people. Maybe all the people. They can't punish all of us."

Duke looked to Willa and shrugged. "It might work."

"How are you going to convince that many people to go along with it?"

"We won't have to. We just need enough to get started. The rest will follow."

Willa still wasn't buying into it. "I dunno, Jane. I just don't think it'll work."

"Why?"

"Your emotions are running unchecked right now. You've got this half-cocked idea and you haven't thought any of it through. What if nobody comes? What if it's just us? We'll all be screwed."

"So you want to just leave Momma Dee up there?" Jane was indignant.

"No, I don't want to leave her up there. But think about it Jane. What you're planning, it could land you right up there with her."

Willa's face flushed.

"I am not going to sit by and do nothing, Willa! I refuse to walk through town and see her up there and not do anything about it." Jane was raising her voice.

"I agree with Jane," Laura finally spoke up. Everybody stared at her. "I can't sit by and not do anything. I can't let Nora and Grace see her like that. We've got to do something."

Duke hadn't said anything during Jane and Willa's exchange. He looked at his watch.

"It's too late to do anything now. It'll be dark in about half an hour. How about this: Jane, you and Maria stay here with Laura. Me and Willa will go out tonight and start spreading the word," he said. Willa opened her mouth to say something but Duke put up his hand. "Only to those we can trust, of course," he added. "If we can get a big enough crowd to start with, like Jane said, the others will follow."

"Especially if you do the same for the others," Maria added.

"That's an even better idea." Duke said. "We'll cut down all of them. Willa, let's go."

Duke stood. Willa hesitated. She looked at Laura. Laura's pleading look was all she needed to agree.

"I've already been to the labor camp one time. Guess I get to look forward to going back." She stood and followed Duke out the door.

It didn't take much to convince Willa's search team to help orchestrate their illicit funeral. Duke and Carlos were disappointed that they were not to be a part of the distraction, which had been decided would involve the stash of fireworks they had been saving for New Year's. Instead, they found themselves standing at the traffic light posts, trying to be as nonchalant and inconspicuous as possible. Duke had had to lock Nuke in the cabin to make him stay home. If anything went wrong, if they didn't make it home, Maria knew to let him out.

Duke stood with Jane and one of the other Searchers, Corey, near the post by the coffee shop. Carlos, Darin, and Willa were at the post across the intersection. Carlos was using the opportunity to flirt with Willa. Jane couldn't hear the conversation, but Willa had her arms crossed and an unconvinced expression. Carlos was getting nowhere, but it didn't seem to faze him. Waiting in the wings were the other guys from the search team with two trucks ready to rush forward at the signal to help.

"So where are they gonna set off the fireworks?" Jane asked.

"They're going to set off in several places down the highway to draw the Guards farther and farther away. Ultimately, they'll finish at the country club."

Jane shivered uncontrollably. She paced in small circles, rubbing her hands across her arms and the back of her neck. She covered her nose and mouth with her gloved hands and blew into them. The warmth of her breath on her nose and fingers was fleeting.

"You cold?" Duke asked.

"No, I'm on v-vibrate mode," she said through chattering teeth. Truth was, she was freezing. The bitter wind bit her face and cut through her layers of clothes. She tugged at the wool headband she had wrapped around her ears. But it wasn't just the cold that had her shaking all over. Just the thought of what they were about to do was enough to nearly send her into a full-blown panic attack.

Just then, there was a rattle of pops and cracks like gunshots down the road. All of the Guards stationed around the square jumped to their feet and took off running. Several trucks tore through town towards the racket.

"Maybe this isn't such a good idea." She looked up at Duke. The grasshoppers in her chest were so familiar, she almost felt the urge to name them.

His eyes widened. "A little late for that, ain't it?"

Another round of fireworks went off; the sound of screaming bottle rockets was further in the distance.

"Well, that's our cue." Duke turned toward the sound of more trucks coming around the platform. This time it was the searchers. Duke bent down and laced his fingers together. "Up you get."

Jane pulled off her gloves and tried to shove them in her pocket, but she fumbled with her trembling hands. One of them fell out on the ground. She put her foot in his cupped hands. He lifted her up so quickly and effortlessly that she felt momentarily weightless. Across the intersection, Carlos had lifted Willa up the same way.

The steel pole was painfully cold, leeching the warmth from her bare hands until they were numb. Jane shimmied the rest of the way up the pole until she was on top of the long arm that stretched across the road. Her ribs were nearly healed, but the effort of climbing sent a sharp pain through her chest. She lay on her stomach, legs wrapped around the arm, and began to pull herself forward as fast as she could. They didn't have much time before the Guards would be back.

Now that she had started, her anxiety fell to the back of her mind. Her nerves calmed. All she could see was the first loop of rope wrapped around the arm in front of her. There were three bodies between her and the first traffic light. Momma Dee hung between the two lights.

Once she reached the first rope, she reached down and unsheathed the long knife that was strapped to her leg. Since she had a free pass to visit her old home, it had been surprisingly easy to smuggle in a few weapons from the root cellar. But she didn't dare bring too much. Each of them had a knife. She'd brought a hand gun for Duke and Willa, but only an extra knife for herself. The knives were necessary for their current plan, but no one but themselves knew about the guns hidden in the crawlspace under the cabin.

The back of the knife was fiercely serrated. She reached around and pulled the serrated edge through the rope just beneath the knot. Duke had personally made sure their knives were sharp. That plus the weight of the body below keeping the rope taught meant that it only took three or four quick pulls to slice through the rope.

The body fell and Jane heard Duke and Corey grunt under the sudden weight. Jane moved on to the next body. The fierce wind gusted suddenly around her, stealing the breath from her chest. She had to stop and cling tightly to the arm of the streetlight to keep herself from being blown off. Her heart jumped into her throat. She began to panic.

"Hey!" Duke called from below. "You remember that time when we were teenagers when dad got those massive damn fireworks and we shot them in November?"

He knew she was panicking.

"The big ones. The—uh—comets," she stammered.

"Yeah. Those big comets. You remember when Uncle Dave knocked it over and it shot right at us? That was some scary shit!"

Jane had made it to the second body and started to saw through the rope.

"Yeah. I remember." Jane had to yell to be heard through the howling wind.

Her fingers were completely numb. It was becoming difficult to hold on to the arm, much less the knife. She dropped the second body and forced herself to move forward to the next.

"I got to thinking," Duke continued his rambling, "can you imagine how freakin' scary it would be if you had that shit shooting at you in, like, a battle or something?"

Jane dropped the third body. She knew Duke's tactic would only work if she participated.

"You mean like as a weapon?" She had come to the first traffic light.

"Yeah. Like a weapon. Like, imagine if you taped sticks to bottle rockets!"

"Dude! That's terrifying."

Duke laughed and waved her on.

She strapped the knife back in its sheath and waited for a break in the wind before she stood up and attempted to move around it. This was the part she had been dreading. The arm was becoming thinner and thinner the farther out she went. It swayed beneath her feet from the wind and her movements. She clenched her eyes shut and wrapped her arms around the light. She put one leg around the light. She felt around blindly for the arm with her foot. When she found her footing, she eased her weight around the light, from one foot to the other. The wind buffeted her with short powerful gusts. The panic began to rise again and scream in fear. She caught a glimpse of the crowd and was emboldened by the cheers and support pouring from it.

Just as she was about to step around the light, an enormous boom rent the air. Jane felt the vibration from it in her chest. Then, off in the distance, a mushroom cloud formed in the air.

"Holy shit!" Jane cried.

"What? What is it?" Duke and the others couldn't see the cloud from their perspective.

"They blew something up."

"That'll be their big finale, I guess," Duke laughed. "You better get a move on. They'll be heading back any minute."

Once she was safely back on her chest and wrapped around the pole, she glanced over at Willa. Willa had had already dropped all of the bodies before the first light and was working her way around the light to the last one. A large crowd had gathered, watching them cut down the bodies. A few of the Guards had returned and were trying to push back the crowd, but five Guards against two hundred people was an exercise in futility.

Jane moved on to the next body. It was Momma Dee. She paused and looked down at the top of her head. Her hair was still up in its clip. It was coming loose, leaving her hair disheveled and falling to one side. She never went anywhere without her clip. Jane remembered how she joked about knowing how hot it was by how soon she had to put her impossibly long hair up.

Any doubt she may have harbored about what they were doing vanished as she watched the body of her best friend spin and sway in the harsh wind. She allowed herself only a single breath to collect herself. She pulled the knife through the rope and noticed it took more effort to cut this time. The knife was beginning to dull. She sawed through the rope in three dragging strokes, sending Momma Dee into the waiting arms of Duke and Corey.

On the other side of the intersection, Willa dropped her last body. She rolled over the arm until she was hanging by her fingertips then dropped into Carlos' arms. People at the back of the crowd began to yell that the Guards were coming.

Jane started to slide over the edge of the arm to hang by her fingers, but her hands were too numb. She lost her grip and fell from the arm with a startled yell. Duke and Corey caught her awkwardly between them.

"Very graceful," Duke said.

Jane couldn't respond. She was too busy trying to calm herself. She just stared at him. Duke settled her on her feet just as the trucks full of Guards pulled back into the square. Jane and her conspirators sat on the tailgates of the two trucks full of bodies. They glared at the Guards as the trucks pulled away down highway 107. The trucks drove slowly so the large crowd could follow on foot. Jane looked at Willa, who sat on the other truck. She lifted her chin.

Stand up with me.

Willa nodded back. *Okay.*

They stood on their respective tailgates. Carlos and Duke grabbed their ankles to steady them. Willa crossed her arms. Jane held her fists by her sides. They stared down the Guards over the heads of the crowd. They knew the Guards couldn't stop a crowd that big. The Guards knew they couldn't. They knew that the Guards knew. They stood defiant, their expressions hard, standing guard over the bodies of their friends, even the ones they didn't know.

The procession had grown to over three hundred people openly weeping for the fallen for the first time. Many of the dead had been there for months, their families forced to see, and ignore, their eviscerated bodies every day. There was another smaller crowd of people that lined the side of the road and watched the procession.

Where the procession was mostly locals, the crowd that watched were primarily the Chosen Citizens, the ones that supported the government and their atrocities. Chosen or local, nearly every eye was weeping. Jane glared at them. How dare they cry on this occasion? They had watched as those people were executed and had done nothing to prevent it. They had stood by and refused to help. But even they could not help but be moved by this show of love and solidarity.

The procession pulled through the Trillium golf course to the one of the greens in the back. The green had been transformed into a massive graveyard. It was the only place big enough to bury the massive number of people that had died in the last four years. The newest graves had been dug at the back of the green by the labor camp. The current labor camp detainees looked up from the graves they were digging to stare at the procession in shock.

The truck drivers pulled up to the nearest empty graves and stopped. They needed to put the bodies in the ground as soon as they could, before anyone stopped them. Several men stepped forward from the procession to help unload the bodies. Sons, brothers, husbands, and friends helped lower their friends and family members into the graves. Someone in the middle of the crowd began to sing a slow, melancholy hymn. The crowd parted around her. She stepped forward to stand near the graves. Many people in the procession knew the song and joined her. It was a despondent chorus of sorrow. Jane's soul ached with loss.

With the pain of their loss was renewed, people sobbed for the people they were not allowed to grieve for before. The Campbells stood in the bed of one of the trucks, watching over everyone, keeping an eye on the Guards that had followed them that now stood quietly at the back of the crowd.

Jane and Willa came down to stand with Laura when they lowered Momma Dee into her grave. Someone had managed to produce a white sheet, with which they wrapped her body. Slowly and carefully, Momma Dee was laid to rest, wrapped in nothing but the clothes she wore and the sheet that was given to her. Someone handed Laura a holly branch, the only pretty thing growing this time of year. Laura reached down into the grave as far as she could and dropped the holly branch onto her mother's chest.

A preacher stepped forward out of the crowd. He did not know many of the people who had been laid to rest, but his eulogy was beautiful and poignant, speaking of the pain of their loss, the future they had helped beget, and the debt they, the survivors, owed them for their lives. He concluded by reminding them that the worst thing they could do was to forget them, to not honor them and the sacrifices they made. He implored them to always remember them, especially in these trying times.

Everyone seemed to draw strength from the preacher's words. The procession, recalcitrant and emboldened by each other's courage, passed the Guards that had followed them without so much as a glance and walked back into town. The crowd dispersed once they made it back to the square. The euphoria of solidarity faded from Jane's heart like a tank of water with a slow leak. By the time she went to bed that night, her righteous outrage had been replaced with anxious dread.

Chapter Twenty-Four

For weeks after the funeral, the entire Village waited with bated breath for the hammer to fall. They all felt it was inevitable that punishment of some kind would be meted out—hangings, whippings, reduced wages or rations—but nothing happened. By the end of January, people began to express cautious optimism that maybe they had gotten away with it. Maybe the Guard had been so moved by the show of love that they had decided to forego any punishment. But many more, including the Campbells, knew that the worst was coming.

Duke had long since given up working at the forge. He worked with Willa and the other Searchers but continued to go to only God knew where at night. Willa had her hands full at the station and helping Laura at the Home. Jane took over the Market, making sure everyone that needed it had something to eat. They were too busy to contemplate Duke's nighttime forays.

The sickness in the Home had begun to spread faster than it could be contained. Some of the children in town had become sick. The local children were sent to the quarantine at the home, but the citizens' children were sent to their own quarantine near the medical center. Every luxury had been afforded to the citizens' children. Each one had their own bed, if not their own room. With ample food and medicine, some of them recovered enough to return to their families. The children at the Home, however, languished on cots lined up in rows in the gym. The fevers and coughs had given way to agonizing headaches and seizures that left the children screaming.

Willa split her time between going on searches for medicine and making repeated requests for it from the guard. The elderly residents refused to take the medicine that was issued to them, insisting that it be given to the children. They stayed and helped care for the children, to their own detriment. Eventually, many of them ended up on cots of their own, fighting for their lives.

"We've issued all that we have, ma'am. Requesting it over and over won't make it magically appear." Willa had gone back to the central office to make another appeal for medicine.

"But we're getting more and more kids every day!"

"That's not our problem. The orphans are wards of the state and we have issued the necessary medication to treat them. If you have more orphans, then you need to register them with the state, and then we can issue more medication."

"But these kids aren't wards of the state! They're children with families! These parents have trusted us with their kids!"

"Then those parents need to pay for the medication they need."

Willa was livid. "You're going to make these people pay? That's bullshit! These people can barely afford to feed themselves, much less pay for medication. What kind of capitalist bullshit is this?"

"A lot of people have put a lot of time, and a lot more effort, into creating that medication, distributing it, and delivering it here. Somebody has to pay them, and the money has to come from somewhere," the Guard replied.

"And your damned government can't take one for the team to save the lives of innocent kids?"

"I'm sorry. There's nothing I can do."

"You're going to pay for this, eventually. I swear to God I'm gonna make you pay for this."

Willa stormed out of the central office but returned to the Home empty handed. She went upstairs to the basketball court. Caretakers and elderly residents moved between the cots, doing what they can to make the children comfortable. A thin woman with thin, straight, gray hair stood and saw Willa in the doorway. She walked over.

"Hey, Karen." Willa was exhausted.

"What did they say?"

Willa shook her head. "There's nothing left. I don't know what to do."

"You'll think of something. I know you will."

"You have too much faith, Karen."

Karen's smile was soft and reassuring. "Honey, all I have left is my faith. When there's nothing left, there is always God. I know you don't share my conviction but you don't have to. I have enough faith for the both of us. He'll show you the way. I know He will."

"Thank you, Karen. Have you seen Laura?"

Karen's smile faded. "She's over there in the corner with Nora."

Willa crossed the court, sticking to the sidelines and away from the cots. She couldn't bear to see the sweating, anguished faces of children who didn't understand what was happening. Laura was sitting on the floor beside Nora's cot. She held Nora's hand, running her fingers across her soft skin. Nora's eyes were closed. Her face in shadow.

"How is she?" Willa knew the answer but the question was habitual.

Laura's face was void of any expression save for the tears that streamed relentlessly down her cheeks.

"Better."

Willa's eyes widened. "Really? I didn't expect—" Then she understood. Nora's chest wasn't rising and falling with her sleeping breaths. It was still. Willa could see now that it wasn't shadow but the fading gray of lifelessness.

Laura's shoulders began to shake. Her chin trembled. Willa knew that she was about to lose it. She grabbed her hand to lead her outside. The last thing they needed was for her to go to pieces and frighten the other children. She pulled Laura to her feet, but the sudden contact seemed to bring Laura back to herself. She collapsed back down to her knees and began to howl.

Willa stooped and wrapped her arms around Laura. Karen and several others rushed over. They laid Nora's sheet over her face, lifted the cot with her on it, and carried her out. Willa clutched Laura tight, as if she could hold her together as she fell to pieces. Children all across the room caught the sense of desperation and began to cry. The echoing gym was a cacophony of anguish. Eventually, Laura cried herself out. Willa led her from the gym to one of the classrooms on the first floor. Karen came in.

"Can you watch her for me please, Karen? I've got something I have to do."

"Of course."

Willa stormed into the station, slamming the door behind her. Absolute fury pulsed in her temples as she went into the office and took her frustration out on several drawers and an ill-fated computer screen. Carlos poked his head in the door.

"Hey now, careful. What's got you in a bind?"

She threw open the large cabinet and began pulling out maps.

"Go round up the others. We're goin' on a hunt."

Carlos's eyes lit up. "Finally!" He left and began hollering in Spanish to some of the other guys in the station.

Willa found the map she was looking for. It was the map she had made months ago of the doctor and patient addresses in the neighboring town of Highlands. She had forgotten about it until now, but now that she had it in her hands, this map was her Hail Mary. If they didn't find anything now, it would be over. The kids would die. Likely, with all the travelers passing through the Village, the flu would spread outside town. Many more people would die. But not the Chosen. No. They would be protected. It would be the locals. It would be...

Willa dropped the map. Her heart sank into her stomach. *They're doing this on purpose*, she realized. The Guard didn't run out of medication, they were withholding it. Why, she couldn't fathom, but that was the only explanation she could think of.

A babble of voices began to filter through the open door of the office. Carlos had returned with Duke and the other Searchers. Willa snatched up the map and walked back out into the bay.

"Whatever you were just doing, you're going to have to drop it. We're leaving right now for another hunt." She raised her voice enough to be heard. The crowd fell silent immediately. "The Guard isn't going to be issuing more medication for the kids at the Home. They say they don't have any, but we all know the truth." She paused. "We're going to have to go find it ourselves. We're going to Highlands. Load up."

Within minutes, the entire crew was loaded into two trucks, Nuke pacing in the bed of one of them, and pulled out of the station. Willa turned onto the highway and headed for Highlands but they were stopped at the barricade.

"No one leaves. Sergeant Smith's orders," the Guard said.

"What? Why?" Duke asked.

"You'll have to take it up with him. But our orders are that no one gets in. No one gets out. Period."

With much grumbling, they turned back to the station.

"All of you stay here on standby while I go figure this out. Duke, c'mon."

Duke got back in the truck with Willa and they drove back into town with the intention of going straight to the compound. Fortunately, they didn't have to go that far. Sergeant Smith was walking around his favorite haunt, the platform in the square. Willa stopped short and threw the truck in park before storming out.

"Why can't my crew leave to do a search?" she demanded.

Sergeant Smith approached the edge of the platform and stared down at her.

"Because you are spending more in fuel for your little shopping trips than you find and bring back. The search team has been disbanded. There will be no more search trips. It is no longer a sustainable practice when everything you need is being provided by the Guard." He turned to the square at large and raised his voice so all could hear him. "If anyone is caught leaving the Village without proper authorization, they will be sentenced to a week in the labor camp." He turned back to Willa. "Why don't you go join your sister waiting tables at your friend's restaurant? Oh wait, that seems to be going by the wayside too, isn't it? Now that she's gone."

Sergeant Smith smirked and turned back to his victims on the platform. Willa shrieked in outrage.

Duke put his hand on her shoulder and guided her back to the truck. He drove them back to the station where the team was waiting.

"We won't be going anywhere. There will be no more searches. There is no more search team."

The outcry was instantaneous. Willa held up her hands and tried to talk to them but they were all talking so loudly, she couldn't hear herself.

"Shut up!" she yelled. They fell silent. "There's no—" She took a deep breath to steady her shuddering voice. "There's nothing we can do. If anyone is caught leaving the Village, you'll spend a week in the labor camp."

"Hell, I'll go," one of the guys, John, called out. "We'll sneak out after dark. A week in the labor camp is worth it if we're saving kids' lives, right?"

The group cheered in agreement, but they stopped when Willa shook her head.

"No. Absolutely not." They began to argue, but Willa raised her voice again. "There is no guarantee we'll find anything."

"But we have to resist. They're killing our kids. We have to fight back!"

"How the hell do you expect to lead a resistance if you're in the labor camp digging graves? No. We'll find another way." Tears welled up in her eyes, but she blinked them away, refusing to show weakness. "We have to find another way."

One by one, the guys left, their shoulders sagging under the weight of defeat. No one's shoulders sagged more than Willa's. She walked back to the cabin with Duke. He kept looking at her like he wanted to say something, but he kept his mouth shut. He alternated between looking at her, opening and closing his mouth, then fidgeting with his hat. Jane met them on the porch.

"What happened?" She didn't need to see their faces to know something was wrong. The crushing disappointment hung over them like a pall.

"The Guard is refusing medication for the Home and Sergeant Smith has disbanded the search team. They won't give us medicine or let us go find our own. Those kids are going to die, Jane, and we can't stop it."

Jane rushed forward and wrapped her arms around Willa. She looked at Duke over Willa's shoulder. Duke was still acting shifty, looking at Jane, then Willa, then his shoes.

"What, Duke?" Jane asked.

Willa turned to look at him, too. She finally noticed how bizarre he was acting.

"You know something, don't you?" Willa sounded a little more accusatory than she meant to, but she was desperate for a solution.

Duke looked around him, as if hoping the right words would come ambling up the gravel path. He struggled with himself for several minutes.

"Spit it out, Duke. If you know something, you need to tell us." Jane spoke more kindly and cast a side eye glance at Willa.

"Okay, okay. Listen, I'll tell you, but not now." He stepped closer to them, afraid that someone might be listening. "Meet me at Jane's house at midnight tonight. I'll tell you then."

Jane stared at him suspiciously, but she agreed.

"I've got to go," Duke said suddenly and turned back down the gravel path.

"Where the hell are you going?" Willa called.

He didn't answer and disappeared around the corner. Willa turned to Jane.

"What the hell is his problem?"

"I don't know, but I need to talk to you too. I've had an idea." They went in the cabin. "I'm worried."

"Me, too. I don't see how we're going to find the medicine now." Willa sank onto the couch and put her face in her hands.

"That's not what I'm talking about. It's not just the kids who are in danger."

Willa looked up.

"I'm actually afraid for all the other people that live here. The other locals. They're not safe here, not with Sergeant Smith in charge. We need to get them out of here."

"But Jane, this is their home. Your home. OUR home! We can't just bug out and let them have it."

"I know, I know. But we can't stay here either. We're outnumbered two to one at least. Any resistance will be put out like a gallon of water on a single candle. They're just looking for a reason to hang us all and replace us with more Chosen Citizens. We, and the people we care about, will be safer in Blue Valley with Nolan, until we are capable of fighting back and taking our town back."

"Okay, and how do you propose we do that? We can't just load everybody up and say, 'We don't want to live here anymore, okay, bye!'"

"We'll have to smuggle them out."

"And have Sergeant Smith wake up one morning to find that half of his pool of victims has magically vanished into the night? I don't think so."

Jane began to pace the small living room. "We'll do it slowly. A few people at a time. We'll construct alibis, fake deaths, whatever we have to do to get them out safe."

"That's going to take months."

"I know. It'll be very slow and laborious, but I don't know any other way to do it."

"Even if we do manage to do that, what about Nolan? He's going to be pissed if a bunch of people from the Village just show up on his door step."

"Nolan will understand, especially if he knows it's us. We'll send a letter with the first person."

"Out of the dangerous land of the secure and protected Cashiers Village, into the safe hands of the barbarians of Blue Valley." The irony was not lost on either of them.

Willa considered this plan for a while until a thought occurred to her.

"Why us?"

"Hmm?"

"Why is it up to us—me, you, and Duke—to do this? To save these people? Is there no one else in this town willing to do this?"

"There is, but they have homes and families here. They have pasts, presents, and futures here. Whereas we..." Jane trailed off but Willa knew what she was going to say.

"We're the only ones with nothing to lose."

Chapter Twenty-Five

That night, just like they promised, Jane and Willa were at Jane's old house on the other side of the lake. They had had to take a long circuitous route down back roads and through the woods to avoid the roadblock armed with Guards.

They had arrived nearly an hour early, but it was now fifteen after and Duke still hadn't shown up. Thunder rolled in the distance and a freezing, sleeting rain had begun to fall. Jane and Willa retreated into the root cellar hidden behind the garage. They hadn't dared go into the house with any light for fear of being seen from a distance.

Jane had just lit the lantern in the root cellar when she heard the front door of the garage open. Her heart jumped into her throat. Willa grabbed a pistol and chambered a round. She couldn't see into the garage, and there was still the possibility that it was a Guard that had followed them. She heard the cabinet in front of the cellar door move. Jane stood near the door while Willa was on the far side of the cellar where she had a clear shot of the door.

Willa pointed the gun at the door. The door swung inward. Jane's breath caught in her throat, and then Duke stepped through. Jane let out her breath heavily and Willa lowered the gun.

"What the hell is this all about?" Willa asked.

"Okay, listen," he said. "I think I might have a solution to the flu epidemic, but you're not going to like it."

"For God's sake, Duke, just tell us!" Jane was exasperated.

He hesitated. His eyes darted around the dimly lit cellar, looking at Jane, then Willa, then his shoes. Then he looked backward out the door and motioned to someone to come. Willa panicked and raised the gun again. Jane gasped and hurried to the other side of the cellar to stand by Willa. Duke stepped farther into the cellar to make room for his companion. Jane had expected Carlos, or Rhys, or even Nolan. She did not expect...

"Charlie?" Jane and Willa chorused in shock.

"Hi, guys." Charlie looked terrified.

"Um, Willa," Duke said, "the gun? Can you put it down, please?"

"Not until you tell me what the hell she's doing here. Are you out of your damned mind? She works for the Guard and you bring her here to our bunker? What the hell is wrong with you?"

"It's not like that, I swear. Please, just put the gun down and let me explain." Duke held his hands up in surrender and took a tentative step towards Willa.

Willa lowered the gun a fraction of an inch.

"Please. I swear she's not going to betray us. She's going to help us get the medicine."

This got Willa's attention. She stared at Charlie.

"Is that true?"

Charlie relaxed somewhat, but she was still intimidated by Willa. "Yes. I can get you into the compound. I know where the medicine is."

Jane looked at Duke. "How did this come about? How did you find out she knows?"

Duke became sheepish again. "I, uh..." He took his hat off and scratched his head. "I've been seeing Charlie for a while now."

Willa's eyes nearly came out of her head. "You're sleeping with her?"

"It's kind of more than that, but that's a conversation for another day. Long story short, yes. And I told her about what happened with the search party earlier and, well, you tell them, babe."

Charlie took a tentative step forward. When Jane and Willa didn't move, she took it as a good sign.

"The Guard has the medicine you need, but they're

withholding it."

Willa put the gun down, "I knew it. I freakin' knew it!"

"Why? Why would they do that? They know how much we need it." Jane was distraught.

"It's punishment for the funeral you pulled off. So many people were there that day. They couldn't send that many people to the labor camp, or execute them, without completely collapsing the fragile economy. The Village is dependent on the local population to do the jobs the other citizens don't want to do."

"You mean the Chosen Ones," Duke said.

Charlie turned to look at him. "Is that what you call us?"

He nodded. "You were chosen to live here, as opposed to having lived here in the first place."

She lowered her eyes, then looked up at Willa. "Anyway, that's why they're withholding the medication. If they can't punish you…"

"Then they'll punish the children," Jane whispered. "Oh my God."

"That's despicable! How can they possibly think they're going to rebuild this country if they're killing kids?" Willa started pacing the tiny cellar.

"Control the resources, control the people." Jane sat down on a box of MREs.

"Exactly," Duke said.

Jane looked at Charlie. "But you said you know where the medicine is, right?"

"Yes. It's in the Ingles warehouse in the dairy cooler."

"How do you know for sure?"

"I'm at the bottom of the totem pole at the clinic. I'm basically their errand girl. They send me to the compound to replenish our supplies."

Willa was still skeptical. "But how do you know it's the right medicine?"

"Because I was a pharmacy tech. I know what I'm talking about." Charlie was more than a little irritated at Willa's doubt. "I also know how to get in without being seen."

Jane was hanging onto her every word. "How?"

"There's a loose section of chain link fence behind the store. I can give you the Guard rotation schedule so you can get in without getting caught."

"How do you know all this?"

"When I first came to the Village, I was in charge of medical inventory at the compound. I could basically make the inventory say whatever I wanted. So when we got a shipment of, you know, 'organic' medicine, I would adjust the inventory. Me and my friends would go out through the loose fence and, uh, medicate."

There was a moment of shocked silence.

"You are way cooler than I gave you credit for." Willa sat down beside Jane.

"How many other people know about this? I mean, people outside the compound?" Duke asked. He was still standing near the door, leaning back against the wall, his arms folded across his chest.

"Nobody but you guys."

"We can't tell anyone. The more people we tell, the more likely it is to get back to the Guard that we know."

"But how are we supposed to get the stuff if we don't tell anybody? Don't tell me we have to do this alone."

"We're the only ones who know, Willa. And we're the only ones that I know of who have a secret stash of weapons."

"But all three of us will have to go in. One to do the stealing and two for cover. We still need a driver."

"I can drive the truck," Charlie offered.

Duke stepped forward and ran his fingers through her hair. "No, you can't, babe. You can't have any part of this."

"Why?"

"If they even think that you might have had something to do with this, you'll hang, no questions asked. No. After tonight, you have to go back and pretend like nothing happened."

"I'm sure Carlos will help us," Willa said.

Duke nodded. "I'm sure he will."

"It won't be enough," Jane said.

"It should be. Last time I was in there—" Charlie started.

Jane shook her head. "That's not what I mean. I mean, distributing the medicine is all well and good, but it won't solve the problem."

"She has a point. Sergeant Smith isn't going to stop at sick kids. He won't stop until he has complete and total control over the Village," Duke said.

"A man like him, he won't stop at the Village either. Can you imagine him in control of the Campus?" Willa stood back up and started pacing. The very idea of that man made her blood boil.

"I'm sure that'll be the next place on his list. Do you think the top brass of the Guard know what's going on?" Duke asked.

"I doubt it," Charlie said. "Do you remember what Governor King said when he left? They're working to consolidate and create a collective state of Carolina. They're busy working their way East and South. As long as Smith has the area under government control, they're not worried about it."

"They have to be stopped," Willa said.

"No." Everybody looked at Jane. "The idea of a collective government is fine. It's what we all want. It's not the Guard that has to be stopped. It's Smith."

"And how do you propose we do that?" The fire was back in Duke's eyes. Just like planning the funeral, it was a problem to be solved. An obstacle to overcome. A wall to bring down.

"We need help. We need Nolan. We'll steal the medicine, pass it off, and get the hell outta Dodge."

"You know there's like a ninety-five percent chance we're going to get caught, right? There are so many holes in this plan," Willa said.

"What will you do if that happens?" Charlie looked up at Duke.

A mischievous grin crept across Duke's face. "The only thing we can do. Go down swinging."

Chapter Twenty-Six

They couldn't afford to wait and plan their heist. Several more children had already died from the virulent sickness. It was now or never if they were going to save the rest of them.

Carlos jumped at the chance to help. He went back to the Fire Station and opened the bay doors. Nuke was in the bed, chewing on a bone. It had taken a lot of convincing to keep Nuke from following Duke. In the bed, just behind the cab, were three duffel bags. The Campbells had piled their sparse belongings, plus a few select pieces from Jane's bunker, in the bed the night before. They had no plans of returning. Carlos covered it with a blanket.

He grabbed a toolbox and backed one of the trucks out into the parking lot. He popped the hood of the truck and opened the toolbox. There wasn't anything wrong with the truck. He'd just tuned it up last week. But nobody else knew that. He jacked the truck up and rolled underneath it. He let it back down again and leaned over the engine. He loosened a few bolts, only to tighten them up again.

It wasn't exactly late, but darkness fell so early this time of year, Carlos had to turn on the headlights. He grabbed a spare tank from their stash inside the station, but it was empty. He picked up several more, but they were all just as light as the first. He found one about half-full. He wasn't sure if it would be enough to get them down the mountain. He glanced at his watch, 7:45. Shit. He was going to be late. The half-full tank would have to do.

He hooked up the tank and tossed a flashlight into the passenger seat. He pulled out of the parking lot and drove into town, headlights bright, and drove around the platform and down the highway toward the compound. He stopped just before the gas station and got out. Quickly, before the Guards came running, he popped the hood and unhooked some wires and hoses. He propped up the flashlight and was just about to start his farce when several Guards came running down the road.

"What in God's name are you doing?" the first Guard demanded. Carlos shined the flashlight right in his eyes, blinding him.

"Sorry, dude. I've been working on this truck all afternoon. I was just test driving it but it gave out on me again. Piece of shit. I think the carburetor is bad. It'll be a bitch to find another one, but it'll be an even bigger bitch to get this thing back to the shop."

The Guard was a little uneasy. "You need a hand?"

"Nah, man. I got this. If nothing else, I can leave it here til morning. It's not like anybody's gonna steal it." He laughed.

The Guard laughed, too. "I guess you're right. But seriously though, you can't be driving through town after dark like that. Save it for the daylight."

"Sorry, amigo. Thanks for being cool about it." Carlos held out his fist.

The Guard gave him a droll stare but fist bumped him anyway.

"Don't be out here too long," the Guard warned.

"I won't. Thanks again."

"Hey, wait a minute. Isn't that the Campbells' dog?" The Guard pointed at Nuke.

Carlos's heart skipped a beat, praying he didn't notice the oddly lumped blanket. "Uh, yeah. He's grown pretty fond of me since I've started giving him bones."

The Guard considered him for a minute, then shrugged. The Guard waved and led his men back to the square. Carlos looked off in the direction of the compound.

"Bueno suerte, amigos," he whispered, and turned back to the truck.

On the other side of town, Jane, Willa, and Duke slipped between the trees, keeping the buildings within eyesight on their right so they knew they were going in the right direction. The frigid February air sneaked under, between, and through their layers of clothing. They didn't dare wear too much, so they wouldn't be weighed down, but they had to wear enough to keep them from getting frostbitten. Jane flexed her fingers. Her hands ached from the cold. She'd only been able to find one of her gloves. She must have dropped it somewhere.

Maria had procured some ski masks. Even with the masks pulled over their faces, their plain black hoodies, and blue jeans, Jane still worried that they would be recognized. As a group, especially with someone as hulking as Duke, they were hardly inconspicuous.

"Hey, check it out." Duke pulled the bottom of his mask up over his nose so that only it and his mouth were exposed. "I'm Batman," he said in his best Christian Bale impression.

Willa scoffed with amused incredulity. "You're an idiot."

It took them nearly half an hour of trekking through the woods before they reached the fence beside the grocery store. They crouched behind a holly bush and peered through the chain link into the parking lot. The large front parking lot was filled with a fleet of vehicles and lit by several portable light towers. They followed the fence back behind the store. Without the light from the towers, it was much darker. Only a dim yellow light above the back door illuminated the short set of steps leading up to it.

"Charlie said once we're through the door, we have to turn right and it's in the dairy cooler." Duke's voice was less than a whisper. It was a sighing breeze that sent goosebumps scattering across Jane's skin. This was so much more stupid than climbing the traffic light and leading an illicit funeral procession. No. That was stupid. This? This was suicidal. Jane began to tremble. Duke laid a steadying hand on her shoulder.

"It's gonna be up to you to do the burglaring, Mr. Baggins." He teased. "You remember what Charlie said it was called?"

She did. They had decided that Jane would be the one to carry the backpack. Willa and Duke would be her cover.

"You don't have it in you to shoot someone if you had to," Willa had said.

They crept down the fence until they came upon the loose section that Charlie had used when she worked at the compound. Just as they were about to crawl through the fence, two Guards came out of the back door and lit cigarettes. They chatted and seemed to be taking their time with their break. The longer they stood there, the more likely the Campbells would be found.

Willa raised her revolver and leveled it at the head of the nearest Guard. Jane put her hand on the barrel and pushed it down.

She shook her head and tapped her ear. *The sound will echo. Others will hear.*

Willa shrugged. *What do we do then? We can't just sit here.*

Jane put her hand around her neck and pointed at Duke. *Choke hold. We just need enough time to get inside.*

They looked at Duke. He shrugged and nodded. Careful not to touch and rattle the fence, they slid through the gap and approached the two Guards who, by miraculous coincidence, were standing with their backs to them. Jane moved over closer to the steps. Duke wrapped his arms around one Guards neck. The other Guard was much taller than Willa so she leaped up on his back and wrapped her arms around his neck. He twisted and flailed, but she just wasn't strong enough to knock him out. Duke laid his Guard out. Willa began to panic and did the only thing she could think of: with a swift and violent jerk of her arms, his neck twisted and snapped. He fell forward with a crash, nearly throwing Willa off. Jane held the door open and the three of them slipped through just as the first Guard began to stir.

The warehouse was a long room that stretched several hundred yards to the left. The cooler that Charlie mentioned was just in front of them. They were alone, but their luck wouldn't hold out forever. Someone would find the dead Guard soon and they needed to get out before they did.

Willa went into the cooler with Jane while Duke stood outside holding the door open, watching the long narrow warehouse. The medicine was in a cardboard box on the right wall near the door. Jane pulled off her backpack and set it open on the floor. She placed handful after handful of vials and syringes in the bag. It wasn't a big bag and didn't quite hold all of it, but it was still more than the Guard had issued in the past two months.

Jane shouldered the backpack and shut the cooler door. She winced as it closed with a loud CLICK. Willa was cagey and on edge. She kept her gun pointed down the long corridor. Jane's hands trembled to the point of uselessness and her heart felt like it would bruise against her ribs. They made it back out the door and down the steps when Jane stopped short. In the bright light of the towers around the far corner of the building, long shadows were crossing the ground. Someone was coming. They were still a good thirty yards from the gap in the fence. Jane wasn't sure if they'd make it, but they didn't have a choice. They ran for it.

Jane breathed a sigh of relief when they made it through the gap unnoticed. They crept back to the holly bush just in time to hear the coming Guards find the body of the one Willa had killed.

"They've got to be around here somewhere. They couldn't have gotten far. And you're sure you didn't see anything?"

"I swear to God." The second Guard's voice was raspy and harsh. "It was like a couple of damned ninjas."

The first Guard sighed impatiently. "You're such an idiot, Bubba."

The Guards began to walk away. They had gotten away with it. They crept out from behind the holly bush, heading back the way they came. They had actually managed to sneak in and—

Willa sneezed.

"What the hell was that? Who's there?" A sudden bright light flooded over them.

"Son of a—" Jane muttered.

The Campbells took off at a dead sprint down the outside of the fence. A great cacophony of noise began as the Guards who saw them began to raise the alarm. Guards came running across the fenced in parking lot, firing at them through the fence. They cut across the road that led to the back parking lot and through the trees to the main highway. Just as they broke through onto the pavement, a horde of Guards came racing through the gate, led by none other than Sergeant Smith himself.

Duke and Willa stayed behind Jane, turning and firing wildly behind them. Ahead of them a pair of taillights and an open tailgate waited for them. Jane didn't stop running as she pulled the backpack off and hurled it into the ditch. A dark figure darted out of the shadows, snatched up the pack, and stole away into the night.

A barrage of bullets rained around them and shattered the back window of the truck. Nuke barked wildly from the cab. He tried to climb out of the busted back window, but Carlos pulled him back in. Jane leaped into the bed of the truck without breaking her stride. Willa followed, landing nimbly beside her.

Duke let out a strangled cry and crashed into Jane, pinning her to the floor. "I've been shot. Oh, fuck! I'm hit."

"Drive, drive, drive!" Willa ducked down and yelled at Carlos. A searing pain sliced across her cheek. She clutched her face and felt her fingers coated in blood. It burned like the fires of hell, but it didn't seem to damage anything beyond repair.

Carlos laid on the gas and tore down the highway. The tires squealed as they struggled to gain traction. Duke stood on his knees facing the open tailgate. He fired his pistol at the shrinking shadows that were the Guards. Bullets continued to fly past their heads as they fired back. A sudden *thwack*, and Duke fell backward onto Jane with a strangled cry.

"Oh shit!" he bellowed.

Adrenaline pulsed through Jane like an electric current as she tried to free herself from beneath Duke.

"What the hell, Duke? Get off."

He cried out in pain and rolled sideways. Jane twisted out from underneath him, putting her hand on his back to push herself up. She couldn't see her hand in the darkness, but she felt wetness.

"I need a light. NOW!"

Willa fumbled with her bag as they barreled down the road. It was all they could do to maintain their balance as Carlos slingshot around the platform and down the highway. Willa clicked on the high-powered flashlight, flooding the bed of the truck in white light. Willa screamed.

Blood was spreading from a dark spot on his back, just below his collar bone. Jane ripped off her hoodie and wadded it up against the growing crimson stain on his back, relying on his own body weight to keep pressure on it. Nuke pawed at the edge of the window, desperate to climb in the bed of the truck with Duke. Carlos pulled him back in again. Nuke yelped as the broken glass sliced his leg and paw. Bright crimson blood stained his white fur.

Duke pulled the ski mask off. Beside him, he found his hat. He laid back against their pile of stuff and settled the hat on his head. "Just like I said. Go down swinging."

Jane used her knife to cut away his hoodie, revealing his white t-shirt beneath. The front was so much worse. A ragged hole in his shirt revealed a massive gaping hole in his chest. Blood flooded from the ragged flesh. Pink bubbles formed as the blood pumped out. The bullet had pierced his lung. Duke looked down at his own wound. He seemed oddly detached, like it was a cool looking prosthetic.

"Oh my God," he muttered. His mouth began to fill with blood. "Oh my God."

Willa screamed again. It was all Jane could do to maintain her composure, and Willa's screaming was not helping.

"Stop screaming." Jane reached out and slapped her across the face.

Willa shrank back against the cab, Duke's blood smeared across her face. She was shaking all over, gasping and sobbing, but she kept the light trained on Duke and Jane.

"Your jacket, Willa. I need your jacket!" Jane screamed as she jammed her fingers into the wound, trying to stem the flow of blood. Duke bellowed and writhed.

Willa dropped the flashlight in her haste. The light danced and pointed into the cab leaving Jane in darkness again. Bright spots danced in front of her eyes from the sudden loss of light. Disoriented, she fumbled the hoodie when Willa tried to hand it to her. She grabbed hold of it and pressed it against Duke's shoulder without taking her fingers out. Jane looked up at his face. He was ghostly pale, but Jane knew it wasn't just the odd angle of the light. His eyes held a fear that Jane had never seen before. The presence of his fear amplified her own. Willa picked up the flashlight again and trained it back on her siblings.

"It's gonna be okay, Duke," Jane cried over the roar of the wind around them. "I got you. You're not going to die. Not tonight."

He adjusted the hat on his head. "It's okay. I'm not afraid."

Jane stared at him, pleading with him, "Don't talk like that. Duke? No, Duke. Stay with me. DUKE!"

Somewhere, deep down inside, she knew it was hopeless. She let go of the shirt. His chest stopped rising and falling. She grabbed his face in both blood covered hands.

"DUKE. NO. WAKE UP! WAKE UP GODDAMNIT!"

Duke didn't respond. There was no life in the eyes that looked at her. She screamed.

Chapter Twenty-Seven

Carlos didn't stop until they were halfway down the mountain. They couldn't go straight to Nolan. The truck was running on fumes. It wouldn't make it to Blue Valley even if they tried.

Carlos found a steep driveway that led down to a house deep in a hollow. When he finally stopped, it was barely 9:30. The oppressive darkness was interrupted only by the headlights and Willa's flashlight. He killed the engine. The headlights went out and the darkness closed in on them. He got out to see Duke lying against the pile of duffle bags. His head slumped forward, his chin resting on his chest. Everything around him was soaked in blood. Willa was still against the cab beside Duke, her fingers frozen around the heavy flashlight. Jane hadn't moved. She was still on her knees, staring at Duke's lifeless body, a thick, sticky layer of drying blood coated her chest and arms.

Willa moved first. She looked at Carlos, who had turned pale and green. He didn't realize the extent of the carnage he was hauling down the mountain. Willa vomited over the side of the truck. Carlos shook himself into action. He pulled a heavy, wool Army blanket from behind the bench seat.

Willa began to sob. "No," she said. "No, no, no." She crawled forward and grabbed his face. His head bobbed lifelessly on his limp neck. She crawled frantically across his body and began chest compressions.

"Help me dammit!" she screamed.

Jane didn't react in the slightest. She was still staring at her brother's body, unable to comprehend what had transpired. Carlos reached up and put his hand on Willa's shoulder. He tried to put the blanket around her. She shoved him away and continued trying to revive him. Reluctantly, she gave up. Her chin trembled as she fell backward and sat at his feet. She put her head in her hands and sobbed.

Carlos turned away. He felt like a Peeping Tom, watching something he shouldn't have ever seen. He pulled his rifle out of the cab and walked up to the house to check it out and see if the door was locked. The house was open and there was a propane tank on the grill on the back porch. He took the tank and hooked it up to the truck. Anything to keep himself busy. He turned the key, but it wouldn't start.

"C'mon," he pleaded but the truck just whined and clicked. He got out and approached the sisters.

"Something's wrong with the starter. Why don't ya'll go inside while I try to get it started."

"Jane," Willa said softly. She was shivering hard from the cold. "Jane l-let's go ins-side."

Jane finally turned at looked at Willa.

"J-Jane, we ne-eed to go ins-side."

Jane didn't respond. She turned back and stared at Duke.

"C-can you h-help us move Duke inside?" Willa asked Carlos.

"No," Jane said.

"Are you insane?" Willa demanded.

"No, he has to stay outside."

"Why?" Willa looked at Jane as if she had completely lost her mind.

"He has to stay out here where its cold. If he gets too warm, he'll...he'll decompose."

"But Jane," Willa sounded concerned now. "Jane, we have to bury him."

Jane turned fully to Willa, becoming animated. "And just how do you expect to do that, Willa? Its fifteen goddamn degrees out here. The ground is frozen solid. At most, we might find a shovel. A pick axe if we're lucky. Do you want to dig a six foot grave out of the frozen ground with a shovel?"

Willa was taken aback by Jane's outburst.

"No. We have to get him to Nolan. He has an excavator. Besides, I-I can't leave him here. Not at some strange house on the side of the mountain. Not somewhere that isn't familiar. Not somewhere that isn't home."

Jane started pulling the duffel bags out from underneath him, throwing them aside in frustration. Her racing mind was trying to comprehend the enormity of what had just happened, but at the same time, it could not, would not, fathom it.

"What are you doing now?" Willa was disturbed by her sister's behavior.

"Freezing temperatures. Rigor mortis. Do you want him to be stuck like this?" She grabbed another handful of stuff and heaved it out onto the ground.

Willa and Carlos moved to help Jane lay Duke out flat in the bed. At six-foot-five, he was too long for the bed. Once they got him laid out, Willa folded his hands on his chest and closed his eyes. Jane looked at him and cocked her head to the side.

"What?" Willa asked.

Jane reached up and touched his face. Reverently, she turned his head to the side. She left one hand on his chest but put the other down by his side. It was how he always slept.

Carlos took the bloodstained blanket covering their bags and draped it over his body.

Only then did Jane realize how cold she was, how hard she was shivering.

Only then did she notice that it was beginning to snow. Thick heavy flakes floated and flurried around them as the wind began to pick up.

Only then did she follow Willa inside. They sat on the couch without looking at each other. Willa reached out and grasped for Jane's hand. Jane took it. They held each other, each of them lost in their own grief. Willa laid over in Jane's lap and cried, her body heaving with her sobs. Jane was shocked into silence. How could this have gone so horribly wrong? Her anxious mind had shut down. It refused to feel anything but disbelief. Despite having watched it happen, despite being covered in his blood, she could not believe he was...

He was supposed to be invincible.

Her fingers brushed the gash across Willa's cheek, making her recoil.

"I need to clean that up," Jane said, grateful for the distraction. She wandered into the bathroom, looking for bandages.

After an hour of trial and error, Carlos climbed back into the truck and tried the key. Finally, the truck roared to life. He sighed in relief. All of a sudden, the wind died. Snow continued to fall. Nearly half an inch had already accumulated. An overwhelming silence fell over the yard. Off in the distance, the silence was broken by a barking dog. It took a moment for the sound to register with Carlos. It wasn't so much a bark but more of a howl. No, baying. A hound was baying. Wait, several hounds were baying. His eyes widened in sudden realization. He leapt to his feet and sprinted back to the cabin.

He crashed through the front door.

"We gotta go. NOW!" He said.

Jane and Willa jumped up from the table, where Jane had been cleaning Willa's face.

"Dogs. They've got hound dogs. They're coming for us!" Carlos gasped.

They ran outside and toward the truck. They threw themselves in the cab just as a Jeep full of Guards came barreling down the driveway. The Jeep's headlights reflected on the fresh snow, blinding them. A pack of hunting dogs came howling out of the woods. Just as Carlos started to pull away, Jane cried for him to stop. She flung the door open and got out.

"What the hell are you doing?" Willa was hysterical.

Lying off to one side was Duke's Panthers cap. Her fingers latched around the hat just as one of the dogs latched onto her leg.

"JANE!" Willa screamed.

Jane managed to kick the dog away, but she was soon surrounded by four others. Nuke managed to free himself of Willa's grasp and leaped into the fray. He grabbed one of the dogs in his jaws and thrashed. Another dog leaped on his back and sank its teeth into his neck. Nuke snarled and reached around to bite it.

The Guards had managed to catch up and were running across the yard toward her. Desperately, she kicked her way past the dogs and managed to leap into the bed of the truck. Seeing that she was free, Nuke wrestled past the dogs and tried to run to the truck. The hounds jumped on him again. Nuke freed himself again and ran into the woods, leading the dogs away.

Carlos lurched forward just as a Guard latched onto Jane's wrist. She overbalanced and fell out of the truck. The Guard threw her on the ground and planted a knee in her back.

"Go!" she yelled. "Just go!"

Carlos didn't stop. He tore out of the driveway, leaving tire tracks in the deepening snow. Willa leaned out the back window and screamed.

Acknowledgments

I want to thank all of my friends and coworkers who listened to me endlessly go on and on about my ideas, epiphanies, and trials and tribulations throughout the process of creating this book. Thank you for listening to me, despite having no idea what I was talking about. I would also like to thank my bosses, Glenn and Kim, for being so supportive of my goals and future enterprises. A special thanks to my project manager, Kristin Perry, for helping me with the logistics of publishing. I could never have done all that alone.

To my artist, Brian Ortiz, for all of his advice, encouragement, patience, and talent. Thank you for bringing the Campbells to life.

To my husband, my deepest gratitude for your love and the fact that you love frozen pizza; thank you for your unwavering support of my dreams. I can't wait to chase this dream with you by my side.

And perhaps most of all, to my brother, Matthew, for helping to shape the character of Duke Campbell and being my sounding board. This book absolutely would not have happened without you.

About the Author

Writer, blogger, and general hippie, A.J. Stewart writes for a local magazine and her blog, *The Survivalist Writer*. When she's not writing the sequel to Hey, Brother, she can usually be found reading Douglas Adams, gardening, or elbow deep in a thrift store somewhere.

A.J. lives in Western North Carolina with her husband and her dog.